The
Crowded
Beach

The Crowded Beach

Laurene Kelly

SPINIFEX

Spinifex Press Pty Ltd
504 Queensbury Street
North Melbourne, Vic. 3051 Australia
women@spinifexpress.com.au
http://www.spinifexpress.com.au

First published by Spinifex Press, 2001

Cover design by Elizabeth Dias
Edited by Barbara Burton
Page design and typesetting by Palmer Higgs
Typeset in Stone Informal and Tekton

National Library of Australia
Cataloguing-in-Publication data:
Kelly, Laurene, 1954– .
The crowded beach.

ISBN 1 876756 06 3.

I. Title.

A823.3

Made and printed in Australia by Australian Print Group

Tasmania

ARTS TASMANIA

Australia Council
for the Arts

The Crowded Beach was assisted
through Arts Tasmania by the
Premier, Minister for State
Development.

This publication was assisted by
the Australia Council, the
Australian Government's arts
funding and advisory body.

CHAPTER 1

Saturday Morning

We've been living at Bondi for five months, my brother Toby and I, with our Aunt Jean. I'm sort of an orphan. My father is still alive, but I like to think he's dead. My mother and youngest brother and sister were killed. I don't like thinking about it and definitely don't like talking about it. I go to this counsellor, so does Toby, and I suppose it kind of helps sometimes. The counsellor says I ought to talk about it, not bottle my feelings up, but sometimes I feel nothing at all. My friends who know me live thousands of kilometres away, and my new friends don't know anything about my past, and I'm scared if I tell them they won't like me.

I'm the only person in the world, apart from Toby, who has a family like mine.

I lay on my bed thinking it wasn't fair. I punched the pillow.

'What are you doing?' Toby's voice interrupted my pounding.

I hadn't heard him come into my room; I nearly jumped out of my skin. 'You should knock, you scared me.' I glared at him. 'What'd you want?'

'Nothing.'

'Well, why are you here?'

'Dunno.'

Gee, Toby was exasperating sometimes. 'Well get out.' I pointed to the door.

'You got your period or something?'

'Shut up, Toby.'

He went out, slamming the door so hard that it shook the things on my dresser. I raced out after him.

'Toby,' I shouted.

He was standing at the window in the lounge room, looking out to sea.

'Listen here,' I said angrily, 'don't come into my room without knocking and don't slam the door. Got it?'

There was no response. 'Toby!'

He turned around and tears ran down his face. Gee, this was the first time I'd seen him cry for ages. Toby tried to speak but couldn't. I felt my own tears and tried to hold them back.

'Jules,' he finally managed to say. 'I want to go home.' Toby sat down and put his head in his hands and I could tell he was seriously crying.

I felt a pain that I couldn't explain. I went over

and hugged him, and couldn't think of words to say, so we cried together, rocking back and forth in our own little worlds. I tried to tell my counsellor once that there weren't words to describe how I felt, and she said I should try and draw it. Weird. How do you draw feeling numb and ashamed for not doing anything to stop your mother, brother and sister from dying?

Why am I alive when they're all dead? Maybe that's what I could draw, me next to three coffins, two of them child-size. Tears got stuck in my throat and I felt a headache starting in the back of my neck. Stinging tears came into my eyes and I couldn't see clearly, everything became a blur. I couldn't comfort Toby; I couldn't even comfort myself.

After a while, Toby and I stopped hugging and sniffed, a bit embarrassed that we'd been so close. I walked over and smelt the flowers in a vase on the dining-room table. I breathed in their scent, it reminded me of Mum. She'd loved flowers. Red and lemon-scented gum flowers, with some green bottle-brush in the middle. I picked a leaf from the lemon gum, crushed it and smelt fresh air, a faraway water-hole, and flowering trees that were gone forever. Trees mum had planted outside our house that had struggled to grow in the dry land. It also reminded me of the waterhole I'd swum in. For a moment everything seemed to stand still, as if the world had stopped. I shook my head to be normal again.

'Do you want something to eat?' I asked Toby who was sitting on the couch staring at nothing.

'Not hungry,' he mumbled.

'Just some toast or something.'

'I'm not hungry.'

'I'm making some anyway.' I went to the kitchen.

I opened the fridge door and resisted eating a chocolate biscuit as I got the bread for some toast. I'd eaten a whole packet of chocolate biscuits once and now was sure I could hear my mum groaning angrily at me, from her grave. I'd felt bad but just couldn't stop myself and before I knew it the packet was empty.

Aunt Jean said it was discipline, that I had to discipline myself. I hated that word; it was one of Dad's favourites. Discipline was whipping your legs with a stick; Toby and I called it doing the Mexican Hat Dance. He said a good belting never hurt anyone. I once answered back by saying he could say that because he was doing the belting and then took off as fast as my legs would go and stayed out till after dark. Dad was drunk and snoring when I snuck back and must have forgotten it by the next day, because he never said anything more about it.

Dad said his father had belted him and it hadn't hurt him, in the long run, and it made him the man he was today. He didn't notice me shudder. I know Aunt Jean was talking about self-discipline, but when I hear the word I can't help thinking about Dad. I'll have to make-up a better word for me not pigging out.

I used to live on a sheep farm, way out WoopWoop, beyond the back of Bourke. It seems a lifetime ago. I used to ride my bike to the bus stop, a couple of kilometres along a dusty red road, to catch the school bus. I now live in a block of flats, on the third floor. I don't have a bike here, I just walk down the stairs, out the door, down the road a hundred metres and I'm at the bus stop. The buses here are always crowded, and I'm so glad I don't have to face that every morning while we are on holidays. If any parent wants to know why their kids don't want to go to school of a morning, just catch the bus with them, I think it will make everything clear. I come home every day with bus bruises. Some bus drivers sure don't like schoolkids. Once, the driver grabbed my bag and threw it off the bus because I'd put it in the doorway when I went to find my bus pass. I'd felt so embarrassed when everyone laughed at me. I miss Mr Simpson our old bus driver, he was never rude to me.

I buttered the toast. 'Are you sure you don't want some toast?' I called out to Toby.

He wandered in and looked in the fridge.

'Do you want to come for a swim?' I asked.

'Dunno,' he shrugged and shut the fridge door.

'We'll feel better,' I sounded like an adult. Yuk, more and more I felt like I was saying things to Toby like Mum would have said like, Change your clothes, Comb your hair. I even was beginning to say some of her favourites, like, A smile exercises more muscles than a frown and, Manners never hurt anyone. I couldn't remember what her voice sounded like, but I just felt every time I said it, that it was really Mum saying things through me. Weird.

'You know what I want?' Toby asked.

I looked at him. He was mussing his hair and sort of pulling it.

'I want everything the same as it was,' Toby said, angrily.

'You know it never can be, Tobes,' I said quietly.

'Why can't it be?'

'Toby, what's happened has happened, we can't change the past.'

'I want to go back home, why can't I do what I want? This place sucks, it's a total nightmare.'

'This's home now, I don't know if you've forgotten or what, but remember what our old house looked like the last time you saw it? Burnt ashes and twisted metal, I call that a nightmare.' The truth is our last home hadn't been that great, but I knew he didn't mean back with Mum and Dad fighting and Dad's drinking.

He meant back in the country, you know the bush, rather than the confusion and noise of the city. Toby said he'd rather be in a real jungle with lions than in a city they called the concrete jungle. It was strange how I was sort of getting used to the millions of people, the noise and the rush, like I'd lived here all my life. I wasn't adjusting to the smell so well, or the constant rumble of traffic. I'd get used to it eventually but, like Toby, I missed the quiet of the country and my friends.

I sighed. Don't get me wrong, I wouldn't swap places now. I loved the bigness of it all, yet really it was small. In fact, the area I live in now, is smaller than our farm but here there are thousands of shops, all kinds of different-looking people and all these different languages, instead of thousands of sheep and lots of red dirt.

'I hate this place. I hate Aunt Mean-Jean. I hate school. I hate everything.' Toby went and kicked the side of the couch. God, his moods changed fast.

'Even me?' I asked.

'Sometimes,' he said fiercely.

7

'Why do you hate me? What have I done?'

'You don't like me any more and you and Aunt Jean gang up on me coz you're girls. You don't care what happens to me, you're always saying do this, do that, all the time.'

'Toby, don't be stupid!'

'Everyone hates me,' he started crying again. 'I hate everyone. I want Mum. I want to go back and live in the shearing shed coz that didn't burn down, the fire didn't touch it.'

'Toby, don't be ridiculous, it annoys me when you say stuff like that, it sounds like you're Crazy King Fruit Loop, come on now, who'd live in a stinking shearing shed?'

'I would, it'd be better than here with Aunt Mean, she's a bitch.'

'She's not, she worries about you. You can't take your bad feelings out on her Toby, it's not fair.'

'She nags me and picks on me all the time, and so do you.' His blue eyes were defiant, and he stared at me with hostility.

This was going nowhere. The chip on his shoulder was growing, not shrinking. I knew he resented Aunt Jean and me telling him what to do, but we had to, otherwise he'd starve to death and become blind from playing computer games for hours.

'Toby, what is going on? Why are you like this?

One minute you seem sad and then you suddenly become really angry, mostly at Aunt Jean,' I waited for him to answer.

He remained quiet. Occasionally he sniffed. I wasn't going to break the silence. My mind was chaotic with thoughts banging into each other, I just wanted things to be better and wondered if Toby and Aunt Jean had fought before I got up. I stayed quiet.

'It's the holidays and there's nothing to do,' Toby finally said.

'That's not what's up and you know it, you can't fool me. What about the beach, you know the one across the road? Was there a beach back home? No! Could we swim every day? No!' I looked at him. 'Are you listening? Remember back home there wasn't enough water in our dam for a frog to swim in.' I dragged him by the ear to the window. 'Look outside here, a great big bloody ocean of water.'

'I'm sick of all that water and sand.' He pushed my hand away.

'Toby, don't be ridiculous.'

'Have you got your hat, your sunscreen?' He mimicked Aunt Jean's voice. 'I'm sick of it!' Toby stamped his foot and walked angrily, through the dining room to the lounge room, and picked up a framed photo from the wooden cabinet that

Aunt Jean said our great-grandmother had brought from Russia.

Toby studied the photo. 'We didn't wear sunscreen at home,' he said quietly.

'We wore hats,' I said gently, 'we always wore our hats.' I knew the photo he held was of Mum, Jonathon and Jennifer, taken when Mum had come home from hospital with baby Jennifer all wrapped up. Jennifer would never grow up to say, Is that what I looked like when I was a baby? I felt the tears start and wondered when would I be able to look at their photo without crying? How long does grieving last?

I glanced at the photos hanging on the walls; my favourite is of Mum and Aunt Jean sitting on the beach when Mum was fifteen, the same age as I am now. The bathers they wore looked sort of the same as now, but their hair was really different. Everything of Toby's and mine was burnt in the fire that destroyed our house, including all our photo albums.

My throat tightened as I remembered images of our photos curled up, in the smouldering ash. I fought the tears, welling up. If it weren't for the photographs Aunt Jean had, there wouldn't be anything to remind us of what our family had looked like.

'Let's go for a swim.' I had to get out of this flat; everything felt like it was closing in on me. I couldn't breathe properly. 'What's Aunt Jean doing?'

'Who cares!' Toby flung himself down on the couch.

'Toby, have you thought about finding out if you can go and stay with someone, you know, like Mrs Thompson, or someone?' I paused. 'I mean, you know Ruby's coming here for some of the holidays, maybe you could go there.'

'See, you *are* trying to get rid of me!'

'Toby, I only mean for some of the holidays, you know going to the waterhole, seeing your mates, that's what I mean. I was only trying to think of something that'd make you feel better. We can't be sad forever, Toby.' I took a deep breath, 'You know Mum would want us to be happy.'

'Poor Mum,' Toby whispered, 'poor, poor Mum.'

'Poor everybody,' I said, thinking of my whole family. 'Come on, Tobe, how about it?'

'Do you reckon Aunt Jean will let me?'

'If that's what you want, I reckon she will.' I shivered. I didn't want to go back there ever, even if someone offered me all the money in the world. 'Do you reckon you can handle it?' I looked at his reflection in the mirror on the wall. Our eyes met. We stared at each other silently.

'What'd you mean?'

'We've only been back once and that was the funeral, and we stayed one night, remember.' I looked away.

'I don't remember much, just lots of people coming up and saying how sorry they were, I don't even remember who they were.' Toby put the photo down and went back and stared out the lounge room window. 'Let's go for a swim, wash our troubles out to sea, forget about all this shit, and be free,' he rhymed, throwing his arms in the air.

'Toby?' I sounded angry.

'Yes?' He looked puzzled.

'Don't swear.' We both laughed.

'What about . . . you know?'

'What?' I'd no idea what you know was.

'You know . . .'

'Toby, I don't know.'

'About me going for the holidays, will you ask?'

'Ask yourself,' I said firmly.

'What if she says no?'

'What if she says yes?' I smiled at him.

I went into the kitchen and put the kettle on.

I like how there are no doors between the lounge room, dining room and kitchen. It's sort of like one big room. It's so different to our old home where the kitchen and everything was separate. Here, the

12

lounge room and kitchen face the sea. It's sort of like the front of the flat even though there's no front door down to the street. There's a little balcony off the lounge room with these big glass doors. The windows above the sink in the kitchen look towards the beach. We live at the Ben Buckler end of Bondi.

Aunt Jean came in with a basket of clean clothes, and began sorting them out. She must have been up on the roof doing the washing. As she put the tea towels in the drawer, Toby got in her way.

'Toby?' Aunt Jean spoke gruffly.

'Yes,' he mumbled.

'Do you want something? You seem to be hovering about like a mosquito.'

Toby looked at me for help. I shook my head. 'Please,' he whispered.

'Oh, all right,' I whispered back through gritted teeth.

'He wants to know if he can go back to, you know where, for some of the holidays.'

Aunt Jean looked at me and then turned to Toby.

'Why didn't you ask yourself?'

'Um . . . because . . . um . . . I don't know.'

'Is that what you want to do in the holidays?'

'Yes.' Toby looked down at his feet.

'Look at me, Toby,' Aunt Jean said.

'What?'

13

'Who would you stay with?' Aunt Jean asked, 'and don't say what.'

Toby gave me a pained look as if to say, see, she picks on me. There were tears in his eyes.

'Maybe Mrs Thompson,' I said wanting to protect Toby.

'Mrs Thompson? That's a good idea, we'll ring her tonight and see if she's willing to have you for some of the holidays.' Aunt Jean's voice was softer. Toby beamed. 'Yes, yes.' He did a little dance where he tried to click his heels, but failed miserably.

Aunt Jean looked at me. I could tell she was concerned and knew she'd want to ask my opinion. It was like that, when Toby was being difficult Aunt Jean would ask my advice on how to handle it. Aunt Jean said I knew him best, but sometimes I felt like I didn't know either of us any more. This was the first time I'd seen him happy in ages. It made me feel good and I smiled at him.

'Let's go to the beach,' Toby said to me.

'I thought you hated the beach,' I said, teasing.

'You sure fooled me, Toby, the way you race into the water and stay in till you come out looking like a prune. If that's hate, show me love.' Aunt Jean laughed and raised her eyes at me.

'I don't like the sand,' Toby said and walked out of the room.

'What do you think?' Aunt Jean asked me.

'He really wants to, he's been a real pain lately.' I paused. 'I know he's sort of homesick.' I stared out the window. Why wasn't I homesick? Was it because I knew our home wasn't there any more? I sipped the cup of tea I'd made. In my mind I saw the flat, red land that had been my home. Paddocks stretching forever with sheep dotted on the treeless dirt. I took in the blue sky, the blue ocean, I could see out the window. It was so different to the red dirt of my past.

'I might speak to his counsellor, and see what he thinks,' Aunt Jean said, as she unfolded the ironing board.

I nodded. 'That's a good idea, he really wants to go, I mean he's nearly thirteen and old enough to know what he wants, I suppose.' I shrugged. 'He's got this thing at the moment, a sort of boy thing if you know what I mean.'

'I think I know what you mean, the great female conspiracy against the weaker sex.' Aunt Jean laughed. 'I think it's best that we find out if it's possible first; you go and enjoy your swim.'

I called out to Toby and he came racing out of his room.

As I walked out the door I thought about how, when I first came here to live, I loved the stairs. It was such a new experience because the only stairs at my old place were up to the verandah and there were only six of them. I'd counted thirty-six to our front door. Toby raced ahead and was waiting for me on the street.

'Looking good, brother,' I pointed at the sea. Our language has changed since we moved here, we say some weird things now. Toby and I talk some common street talk we've learnt at our new school. I like it when Toby and I get on, he can be very funny and he's my only brother now. The people in the streets and on the beach give us something to laugh at together. We just have to look at each other and we know exactly what we're thinking. There are some real fakes out there, the try-hards who'd be better off at home, looking at themselves in the mirror all day, rather than taking up space on our beach. We call them steroid people, they pose on the beach like peacocks and peahens, and they never ever get their bathers wet. We laugh at some of the joggers, and other idiots who meditate and chant and things. I've seen men get dropped off in flash cars at one end of the beach and then they jog to the other and get picked up by someone at the other end. Toby and I have chased joggers, just to annoy them.

We walked down the steps that lead to the north end of the beach where there's a children's playground and wading pools. It was already busy and the beach was filling up. The smell of coconut oil and sunscreen was everywhere. Little dumper waves crashed the shore and the seagulls circled, squawking loudly.

When we first started coming to the beach, we didn't know where to look; some people's bathers were so small you wondered why they bothered putting them on. Aunt Jean said the smaller the bathers, the more they cost. Stupid, eh?

I always try to look straight ahead, but sometimes I accidentally walk into people sunbaking. I was becoming less scared of the crowd but I still wouldn't come to the beach on my own.

We found a small spot of sand between the first set of flags and claimed it with our towels. I ran into the sea, dived under a breaking wave, and came up spluttering. Toby swam past me and I swam after him. We body-surfed the first wave, but I didn't catch it right so didn't go far. Toby went all the way in and was dumped on the shore.

I lay on my back, bobbing up-and-down throwing my arms out, as if I had an audience.

I love lying in the sea watching the sky and pretending that the beach isn't crowded, that it's just me and the ocean. I love the feeling of weightlessness, floating on the waves, imagining another place, another island. I guess I'm sort of lucky, I mean I could have ended up in an institution or a foster home or something. I'm lucky to have Aunt Jean to live with. It doesn't make it any less sad though, losing my Mum and everything. Things can only get better. I sighed and ducked under a big wave.

CHAPTER 2

Saturday Evening

We got back from the beach and Toby ran and grabbed the first shower. There was a note on the kitchen bench from Aunt Jean. I picked it up and read it while I got a drink from the fridge. She'd gone shopping and would be back about five. I glanced at the clock, the one Aunt Jean called her kitsch clock. It's an aquarium clock with these fish that bob up and down, and every hour it plays this fishy little tune. I grabbed my drink and went out on the balcony.

I stared at the beach and wondered if somebody got into trouble in the surf, whether I could save them and be a hero? Aunt Jean had told me how in 1938 there were three freak waves over ten metres tall that washed hundreds of people out to sea, but only a few drowned. Apparently it was lucky that there were heaps of lifesavers there that day. A few years ago, lifesavers rescued a hundred people who got caught out of their depth with the backwash from a freak wave. Aunt Jean drummed into us that we had to respect the sea and not do anything foolish, and how important it was to always swim between the flags. Imagine if it happened while I was sitting, watching. I'd be too far away to do anything.

The beach makes you very thirsty; I suppose it's all that salt water you don't mean to drink. I sipped my iced water noisily because there was no one to tell me off. I felt lonely and maybe slurping noises would stop me thinking about it. I sipped harder. I stared out at the huge expanse of ocean and saw silhouettes of ships against clouds gathered angrily on the horizon. I didn't think the storm would come this way because the sky above me was cloudless and there was only a slight breeze.

I wondered what it would be like to be on a huge ship in the middle of the ocean, or even a small yacht, sailing maybe to South America or one of those small Pacific Islands. You'd be sailing back in time, like when you fly to America you get there before you've left because of the dateline. It'd be great sailing back into the past and changing it as you sailed along.

I wished I had someone to talk to, instead of just myself. Toby wasn't much good and Aunt Jean was too old. I'd had the same friends all my life and had never needed to make new friends till now, and it was really hard. I felt different to these city people, almost like they had a different language and a lot of them did. How could I have known my life was going to change so drastically? Everything I thought I knew was nothing, absolutely nothing. The rules are all so different here, you know it's okay to push and shove and be rude. If people were like that in the country, nobody would ever talk to 'em.

I have nothing to show for fourteen years of my life, no diaries, photos or anything. I felt angry. It's like my past doesn't exist anywhere but in my memories. I thought of my old room and the funny little bed I'd had, with its carved legs. It had been made by Dad's father and was burnt to nothing in the fire. My new bed is metal and will last forever. There are these pot plants on the balcony. I picked some dirt out and threw it over the side without even looking and heard someone say 'hey'. It stopped me from crying.

I sipped harder and wondered if I'd always have the feeling that I could burst into tears at any time, anywhere. Was I going to spend the rest of my life crying for the things I'd lost? The adults don't tell you about the real stuff, like, What happens to us if you die, Mum?' No one wants to think about it, it's too morbid, but then if it happens you don't know what to do, or how to act or anything. We ought to have been prepared because of Dad's violence.

I think Mum thought we didn't know how bad it was. If they fought in the night, Mum thought we didn't hear because we were asleep. If I ever said anything she'd just tell me to mind my own business. I know before Mum died, she'd wanted to change things. Just before it happened, she'd said if Dad didn't get help, we were leaving and she meant it this time.

She used to apologise a lot for Dad, saying it was because he had to fight in the terrible Vietnam War, and that we had to forgive him his nightmares. After a while she stopped saying it, practically stopped saying anything except for when she nagged at us. I sipped the last of my drink and stared at a big boat on the horizon but I couldn't tell if it was going north or south. It seemed stationary. What if it caught fire while I was watching it, I thought, but I couldn't be bothered going to get the binoculars.

I wondered if Mum had left Dad, would she have brought us to Sydney to live? The biggest place I remembered ever going to before here was Bourke. Apparently we used to come here for holidays sometimes when Toby was a baby. I can't remember and my counsellor says that it is easier to remember horrible things than good things, but maybe one day I'll remember good things.

Looking over the balcony, I saw all kinds of people strolling about. Some were looking over the cliff down to the rock ledge and the turbulent sea.

There used to be a statue of a mermaid down there somewhere, but they took it away before the waves destroyed it and it's at the Waverley Library now.

People were walking and fishing from the rock ledge where booming waves crash into the edges and adults and children ran away from the spray, shrieking with pleasure, and fishermen stood there getting drenched. No wonder so many drown.

There were a couple of rescue boats idling on the waves, with lifesavers scanning the sea with binoculars. The boats disappeared constantly in the swells and I wouldn't have been surprised if they ended up rescuing each other.

I looked around to the beach and thought how it's amazing what people wear to the beach. There are some women covered head to toe and others with the barest of string on and men in these pieces of cloth that barely cover their bums while other men wear sarongs or long robes. I wonder if the full robes are cooler than bathers? It's amazing how humans can be so different in looks, food, language, clothes, yet basically get the same pleasure from the beach. They flock here every weekend in the thousands, all laying claim to their own little bit of Bondi. I wish they wouldn't because it's my beach.

I wonder too, what would happen if some of these people moved to the country. It probably wouldn't be very welcoming, especially if they don't speak good English.

The people in the place I'd come from in the country didn't welcome strangers, especially foreign ones. When my Mum moved to WoopWoop, even though she was a schoolteacher, they thought she must have done something wrong to leave the place she was born. That was in the 1970s, and Mum was in her twenties.

Mum told me she couldn't believe it when someone told her that the town was suspicious of her because she wore black socks and jeans. Mum told me that in those days, because she wasn't married, she could be sent anywhere, and that they'd sent her to the biggest hole on earth, and she'd cried every night, for a year. She'd been very lonely and had felt like an alien. She wasn't even really accepted when she married my father, who was a local.

I wonder if she'd married Dad out of desperate loneliness? Mum had lived in that place for more than twenty years, yet I heard an old guy at her funeral say, She always was an outsider, as if that was the cause of her death.

Now I'm an outsider, but maybe my loneliness is different from what Mum's was? After all, there are millions of people here but Mum only had millions of sheep.

I couldn't just sit for the rest of the day. School holidays can get boring, which is pretty funny really coz when you're at school all you want is for the holidays to start and then when they're here you wish you were at school with your friends. I'd sort of made two friends at my new school. I thought they liked me, but I didn't feel like I could just ring them up. I wouldn't have known what to say. I met them when one of the staff introduced me. It was school policy, so you didn't hang about lost, if you were a new kid. I was really embarrassed and felt like such a loser that these strangers were made to act like they were my friends. Their names are Phoebe and Jasmine and they're great, and didn't care where I came from. They're used to new kids coming to their school, because there are a lot of flats in the area and people are always moving in and out. I thought, I bet Jasmine and Phoebe don't sit around bored and miserable like me, I bet they do exciting things in the holidays like . . . like, damn I'm so boring I can't think of anything exciting.

I went inside, got the newspaper, another drink and some biscuits and I took them out to the balcony. I didn't like the front page of the newspaper so I turned the page, and read a headline saying 'World Runs Out of Water'. I read how the world could run out of water in fifty years if drastic measures aren't taken now. I thought the headline meant tomorrow or next week or sometime soon, but fifty years, who cares? I won't even be alive because that would make me sixty-five and there's no way I'm going to live that long to be abused in a nursing home, mugged or bashed because I'm old. No way!

As I ate my biscuit and sipped my drink, I looked out to the ocean. How could the world run out of water? I mean look at all that water out there. I knew they didn't mean salt water, but surely in fifty years technology could figure out how to make the sea drinkable, and because the ice caps in the Artic and Antarctica are melting, couldn't they figure out how to collect that water before it melts into the sea?

I feel a bit guilty about how much water I use, especially in the shower. Sometimes I have these really long showers because I can cry heaps and no one can hear me. I better figure out somewhere else so I don't use more than my share of water. I don't want it to run out before I die. I never leave the tap running, when I'm brushing my teeth.

I turned the page of the newspaper and on page eight there was a photo of my father, handcuffed and being put in a police car. His face had got all little squares over it. I knew it was him. I didn't want to read it. I knew what it was about. Aunt Jean told me it was called a committal, and it's where they'll decide if Dad has to go to trial or not. It happened yesterday, that's why it's in the paper. I didn't look at the words, just squinted my eyes and studied the photograph. I could see his face, sort of. He looked very thin and sort of stooped. I put the newspaper down and put my drink on his face.

I wandered inside picking things up and putting them down. I stared at this painting. It is a print called 'Memory of a Colour Pattern' and was painted by someone called Nancy Guest. It's a pretty busy painting, with lots of women in it. I preferred the one on the other wall called 'Field Naturalists', painted by Jane Sutherland, and went and studied that. There are three children standing in a pond, probably collecting tadpoles or yabbies.

It reminds me of when Toby and I used to catch tadpoles and these insects we called speed boats, that we tried to get to race each other, in our dams. It only happened after a big rain. The picture's background looked nothing like the barren country

I came from; it had wildflowers and colour in it. Our dams were pretty revolting because the sides would have thousands of sheep hoof prints in the cracked earth and no colour, except the murky water sometimes had a green tinge.

I walked over to the wooden cabinet and studied a photograph of my Mum and Aunt Jean standing in the front of the building I live in now. They were in their school uniforms, waiting for the bus. It was Aunt Jean's first day of high school and her eyes were twinkling with excitement. I felt a pang of loss that there weren't any photos of me on my first day at high school that I could look at. It was Mum's fault I thought and slammed the photo down.

My great-grandparents had built the flats as a whole house. Generations of my mother's family had lived here, and when my grandmother married my grandfather they converted the third floor to a separate flat. Eventually the whole building ended up as separate flats, that some people call apartments. Aunt Jean is the only family left, apart from distant cousins, but she owns the building and we are the only residents with a floor to ourselves. The other two floors have two flats on each floor. I hardly ever see the people who live in them.

I sat down on the couch. I could have looked at some of the photograph albums but didn't feel like it. One of my favourite photos is of this elephant on the beach that people used to pay to have rides on. I couldn't imagine an elephant on the beach today, people would panic and there'd probably be a dreadful squashing accident. I miss Mum but felt angry that she hadn't told me about her grand-father's photo albums. Why hadn't she spoken about her mother and father much? Why hadn't she shown us photographs of elephants on Bondi beach?

I put my head in my hands and thought if anyone had told me I'd never see her again, I'd have been nicer to her, helped her more in the garden and not argued about housework or clean-ing my room. I'd have worked harder at school. I'd do anything to see her again, to smell her again. I would kiss her goodnight every night and tell her how much I love her.

I threw myself on the couch. Why, why, why?

I miss Jonathon and Jennifer, my little brother and boo-boo sister. I sobbed remembering the game we played called boo-boo. I slid on to the floor and wept face down on the carpet. I banged my fists on the floor and sobbed. Tears and snot clung to the rug, one of those patterned ones with lots of colour. I looked at the swirls and noticed what I thought was just a splash of colour was actually a bird, a peacock, and then I noticed these figures with gifts and flowers and snakes and everything changed. I stopped crying and rubbed my eyes and wiped my nose on my arm. I looked closer at one of the little figures, it sort of reminded me of Jonathon.

I stood up and went to look in the mirror hanging in the lounge room. My eyes were red and puffy, my face blotchy. Not a good look. I wandered into my bedroom. It used to be Mum's room. The walls are this cobalt blue and the ceiling is quite high. It's got these little decorations around the light and edges called a frieze. I think they are sort of angels or pan pipers or something. They are all different colours. Mum painted them, after a great big argument with her father. Aunt Jean said those two were as stubborn as each other, but Mum usually won the battles.

I looked in my wardrobe at the mirror on the inside of the door. It's one of those full length ones. Staring at myself, I wondered when I'd like what I saw? My hair colour, my eyes, my nose, and my teeth? Was I too fat? When would I shut up with all these stupid questions? Whenever I looked at myself, I saw faults, like my eyes were too far apart, my nose a bit long. Why couldn't I just look in the mirror and say, Hi gorgeous, like my friend Ruby does, every time she sees a reflection of herself. Well she used to,

I wonder if she still does? It felt like ages since I'd seen her.

The phone rang. It'd be great if it was Ruby, I thought as I raced to answer it.

'Hello.'

'Hi! Is that you, Julie?'

'Yes.' The voice was familiar, but I couldn't think who it was, it wasn't Ruby and my heart sank a bit.

'It's Phoebe from school, you remember?'

'Oh, Phoebe. I thought I recognised your voice. I didn't know you had my number.' I felt shy.

'Don't you remember, you gave it to me a few days before school broke up and I told you I'd ring some time.'

'Oh, that's right, I didn't know if you meant it or just said it, you know.' I was blabbering.

'Of course I meant it, you idiot, god the holidays are boring aren't they? I don't know about you but I just sit around wondering what to do and end up doing nothing. My mum reckons I'm in the same place with the same dumb look on my face that I had when she left for work nine hours ago. God, parents can be rude.'

'I know what you mean, but I thought it was just me.' I felt relieved, I wasn't too weird.

'I rang to see if you want to come to this party tonight with Jaz and me?'

31

'A party?'

'Yeah. A birthday party. It'll probably be boring. I don't know if you remember Robbie Johnson, he was going to invite you but forgot.'

'I don't know if I'll be allowed.'

'There'll be adults there. Come on say yes.'

'Well . . .'

'Come on, Julie. It'll be fun.'

'Robbie, which one's Robbie?' I asked.

'You know Mozzie? Blonde hair, big lips, stands real close to you when he talks, spits on you sort of.'

'I don't remember him.'

'Don't worry, he's not worth remembering. Come, we'll look after you, say you'll come.'

'All right, if I'm allowed. I'll ask my aunt when she gets home, I'll ring you back.'

'Your aunt, do you live with your aunt? I wished I lived with my aunt instead of my excuse for a mother, it must be cool.'

I hadn't told Jasmine or Phoebe I lived with Aunt Jean. 'Yeah, my brother and I live with our aunt.' I took a deep breath. 'Our mum's dead.'

'Oh, Julie I'm sorry . . .' There was silence on the phone. 'I didn't really mean that about my mum, not really, I mean she's not too bad, I mean she's not Shirley West or anything.' Phoebe sort of laughed,

32

then spoke softly. 'You didn't tell me about your mum, what about your dad?'

'He's dead too,' I lied and thought of the newspaper and was glad they weren't allowed to print his name, or show his face. It was to protect Toby and me.

'I'm sorry, I didn't know, you never said anything.'

'Well, it wasn't long ago and I still don't like talking about it.'

'Was it an accident?'

How could I answer that? If only it'd been a car accident, not horrible murder.

'Julie, are you there?' Phoebe asked.

'Yeah, an accident.' I answered quietly not wanting any more questions.

'How terrible, you poor thing, why didn't you tell us? I don't know what to say, is it all right, you know living with your aunt?'

'She's okay. She's Mum's sister and in some ways they are a lot alike so it isn't too bad, but I miss my Mum heaps,' I choked. Phoebe didn't seem to notice.

'Well what about the party?'

'If I'm allowed, where is it?'

Phoebe gave me the address and I promised I'd ring her back. I was in a bit of a daze. Me, being invited to a party. What would I wear? I wasn't sure if I wanted to go. I didn't know anyone and what if no one talked to me. Sure I knew Phoebe and Jasmine and a couple of others, but I didn't feel like I belonged. I thought about my friends back home and wished I could see them. I hoped Aunt Jean would get back even though I was a bit confused about whether I wanted to go to the party or not. What would Aunt Jean say? I was pretty sure she'd let me go.

I went and got a book from the lounge room and heard Aunt Jean coming in the door. I raced back into the kitchen.

'Aunt Jean?'

'Yes. Where's Toby?'

'Oh, um, playing on the computer, I think.' I nodded towards his room. 'Aunt Jean, can I go to a party tonight?'

Aunt Jean looked at me with surprise.

'A birthday party, Phoebe rang and invited me,'

'That's great Julie, whose party is it?'

'Oh, some boy called Robbie I hardly know, it's his fifteenth and there'll be adults there,' I said quickly.

'Goodness me, your first party.' Aunt Jean looked a bit uncomfortable. It was like she thought of something bad. 'Where is it?' she asked.

'In Albion Street. I could walk there.'

This time her face looked alarmed.

'Phoebe said it starts at eight,' I butted in, 'but you don't get there till about half-past-nine, if you want to look cool. It goes till about one.'

'I'd rather drive you, if you don't mind, and pick you up. It's not safe around here after dark.' She looked at me. 'When your mother and I were your age . . .' I must have raised my eyebrows or something. 'Julie.' Aunt Jean said in a firm voice.

'Yes? I was listening.' I looked at my nails and sort of whistled silently.

'All I was going to say was that it used to be safer, and that it's fine for you to go to the party when we make acceptable arrangements about you getting there and getting home, okay?'

'Fine, fine.' I stormed out. I don't know why I did, I just did. I stood in the hallway fuming. I wanted to hit something or throw cushions around but it didn't make any sense so I went back to the kitchen. Toby walked in just as I started to apologise.

'I'm sorry, Aunt Jean. I'm really sorry, I don't want to go off like I do, it just sort of happens.'

'You're always going off,' Toby said disgustedly.

'Toby! It's all right, Julie,' Aunt Jean paused. 'I don't want to fight with you, any more than you want to fight with me, but I appreciate your apology, it's a big person who says sorry and means it.'

'I don't want to fight with anyone, it's just hormones or something, I can't seem to help it.'

Toby raised his eyes and pulled a face.

'About this party,' Aunt Jean said.

I hoped she wasn't going to stop me from going because of me going off.

'What party?' Toby asked.

'Julie was invited to a party,' Aunt Jean replied.

'Who invited you?'

'Phoebe.'

'We'll ring and make arrangements, I'll speak to her mother,' Aunt Jean said and walked out of the room.

I ran to the phone. Phoebe was rapt; she'd been to heaps of parties and said if I got to her place about half-past-eight, she'd do my hair. I asked her what sort of present I ought to get seeing it was a birthday party, and Phoebe said most people don't bother getting one, but I could put my name on their card. I handed the phone over to Aunt Jean and raced into the shower.

I thought about the world running out of water and all the people in the future who might never know what a shower was and wondered if other people thought about it. I changed my clothes about a hundred times. I had butterflies in my stomach and felt a little bit sick. A party. My first party in the city.

CHAPTER 3

Saturday Night

I got home from the party at about half-past-one. Jasmine's mum dropped me off. It had been all right, I suppose. I don't know how many kids were there, but it seemed heaps. When Phoebe introduced me to Robbie, I thought, Yuck! and saw why he was called Mozzie, the way he hovered around everyone, getting real close and personal. I lay thinking about the difference between the kids at the party, and the kids I'd known all my life. My life in the bush had seemed so simple compared to here. I could hear the sea and the noises of traffic and it amazed me that so many people were up this late.

I couldn't get to sleep; there was a constant buzzing in my ears. It sounded like an aeroplane about to land but never did. I kept waiting in the dark saying 'land' to the noise, but it wasn't an aeroplane it was the hum of the traffic that never stopped. I thought I'd be tired and would fall asleep as soon as my head hit the pillow. As the party got later, I'd wished that I was at home. I even yawned in someone's face when he tried to kiss me. I don't even know his stupid name. He said I needed some go, and if I wanted he'd get me some, but I just thought he was a nut and told him the only go I wanted was for him to *go* away. He called me something not worth repeating and said I was just a dumb down-country chick, a country bumpkin. The other boys laughed and started hissing and booing so I ran into the kitchen.

The party had been inside and out. The adults were inside drinking alcohol and a lot of the kids were outside drinking alcohol, mostly boys. The adults didn't seem to notice or care, except for Mrs Johnson. Every now and then she'd say to her husband, 'Brian, Brian, do something.'

He'd just wave his arms and say, 'It's a party Marge, for god's sake, relax!'

'But Brian . . .'

'Shut up, Marge,' Mr Johnson said, and I didn't like him.

One of the other women put her arm around her and led her into the lounge room. I wondered if Robert's father had allowed them to have alcohol. Maybe he thought he couldn't sit in front of the kids guzzling back beer, and then saying they couldn't. Maybe he wasn't a hypocrite, like lots of adults. I knew there was no way Mum would have let there be alcohol at my fifteenth birthday. I dunno what

Dad would've done, he probably would've been drunk. I don't think I would have wanted alcohol anyway, it made some people act strange.

Phoebe and Jasmine had told me not to drink the fruit punch. They'd brought bottled water. They said some of the boys poured spirits into the punch so they could get power over girls. I thought they meant, bad spirits, like bad spells or something and I felt a complete idiot when I asked Jasmine about it. She laughed so much she dragged me with her to the toilet, so she didn't wet her pants. I finally got out of her that they meant alcohol, like rum and gin and vodka. When I got over my embarrassment, I made Jasmine promise she wouldn't tell anyone.

I got up, sick of lying in bed, twisting and turning. When I thought about it, I wasn't sure if I'd really enjoyed the party much. I was pretty sure Mrs Johnson didn't know what they were doing to the punch. Mozzie had spewed and I heard him tell his mother that it must have been the cake. I didn't think she was that dumb that she didn't know the truth.

I hadn't been able to sleep because of this image I kept seeing from the party. Every time I'd closed my eyes, I'd seen this very drunken girl, about my age, surrounded by these boys, jeering her to strip. She was swearing at them and falling over. One boy jumped on top of her. The others cheered as they wrestled for a while. Some of the boys said horrible things. I could still hear it in my head. I was scared for her and didn't know what to do.

Actually, I was scared, full stop. The girl tried to get this boy off her, swearing at him, and another boy grabbed her. The girl screamed and screamed. The whole party heard. A couple of the women came out of the house and the boys involved acted like nothing was happening as the girl lay on the ground crying. Some girls went and helped her get up and they yelled, We know who you are, at the jeering boys. When I went inside she was asleep on the couch with a blanket on top of her. I didn't even know her name. I hoped she was safe and had someone watching out for her. It was a horrible scene, worse than television or some movie. I could see the girl's frightened face. It was good she screamed or I don't know what would have happened. I would have had to do something; I couldn't just stand there and watch, or pretend it wasn't happening. But what could I have done?

The sound of people yelling out on the street broke my thoughts. I heard glass breaking. Voices yelling. Did everyone in the world fight? I just wanted to get to sleep. The parties I'd been to in the country seemed so childish now. Everyone singing happy birthday. Blowing out the candles. Playing games like hide and seek. Those days are over and now all I've got to look forward to is loud music, strangers and dangers. I hope I can cope. I'd had my fifteenth birthday quietly here with just Aunt Jean and Toby and I was glad I didn't have a fifteenth party like Robbies'. What a mess!

I wondered if I should tell Aunt Jean about the party, the alcohol and all that. I didn't want her to worry and say I couldn't go to any more. It was a dilemma. Jasmine and Phoebe said it was pretty much like all the parties they went to, except there were more adults at this one than usual. I asked them if there was alcohol at all their parties and they said always and not just alcohol, but drugs as well. I was a bit shocked. Drugs. What sort of drugs? I mean I knew about marijuana. In the country, everyone knew about marijuana. In a small town there was always someone you knew who got busted for growing it or smoking it.

I told them about the boy who tried to kiss me and what he'd said. They'd laughed and told me he was offering me a kind of drug and that I had a lot to learn. I asked them if they had ever tried drugs. They looked at each other before Phoebe said she'd tried some, Jasmine as well. They said it was one of those real no no's that you weren't meant to do and

41

that made you just want to do it yourself, to find out what they were going on about. I was shocked, but didn't say anything, because it all sounded so alien and I felt dumb for asking. They'd asked me if I'd noticed the stoned kids at school. I had to admit I hadn't, they said wait till I was more used to it, I'd get a shock because heaps of kids used drugs at school.

I got back into bed. I didn't want to count sheep to get to sleep, because I'd left all the sheep behind. I wondered what else I could count and remembered someone telling me that if you counted back from a hundred it worked. As I lay there, I thought of all this new stuff to worry about, like as if my childhood was over and now I nearly was an adult and had to face adult things. I shook my head. 'No, I'm not ready,' I whispered to the dark silence of my room. I lay listening to the waves crashing. Always crashing, I thought. Crash, crash, I thought in time to the next waves. I don't know for how long before I eventually fell asleep.

I was woken by a nightmare. There was a fire floating on the water and Mum and the kids were screaming. I could hear my dog Jesse barking as if she were calling to me. I woke up scared and crying, my heart beating at a million miles an hour. I looked at the clock. It said three-fifty-seven. What time did you die, Mum? I asked the void of changing light. I felt a shadow of my mother in the room and searched for something real that would tell me she was really here, but there was nothing. The stars were barely visible high in the sky. I missed the night sky of the country, with trillions of stars above my head as bright as could be, like the Southern Cross, Pleiades and Orion. I wanted to see them again. The shimmering city lights created a buffer between real light and dark and I shook my fist at the false orange night. Who stole the stars?, I whispered to the night sky.

I went back to bed and hoped sleep would come. It must be the party, I thought as I hugged myself tight and tried to think about something good. My eyes stayed open, so I got out of bed and stared out the window. I sat there staring into the night, listening to the sounds of the waves, smashing against the rocks at the base of the cliff. The light gradually started to change as dawn broke. Birds I didn't know lived here started noisily waking each other up. The traffic noises were sort of dull in the background, but I could hear the sandcleaners at work on the beach. I watched, amazed, as the sun became huge as it rose quickly above the horizon at the edge of the ocean. Reds, greens, purples and oranges splashed the sky. Little puffed-up clouds sped along the horizon lined with gold, I took a deep, deep breath.

'I'm going to be the world's champion surfer,' I said to the sky, the sea and to Mum.

I went back to bed feeling sort of happier and fell straight asleep.

Sunday Morning

I think I was awoken by the smell of food. They say it's the last of your senses to respond when you're asleep and that's how come so many people die in their sleep when their house catches fire, they don't smell the smoke. Maybe my stomach woke my brain, because I was very hungry. I looked at the clock. God it was lunchtime. The sky was a cloudless blue with the usual gathering of cumulus clouds on the horizon. No evidence of the light show I saw at sunrise, even the sun seemed different because it looked so small high in the sky. I had to get up and see what was cooking. It smelt delicious.

'Morning,' I said as I walked into the kitchen.

'Good afternoon,' Aunt Jean replied, looking amused.

'Oh . . . well, I couldn't sleep. I saw the sunrise, it was fantastic, so many colours, I'm going to paint it one day.'

'No wonder you slept late, it must've been the excitement of the party.' Aunt Jean looked at me. 'Did you have a good time?'

45

'Yeah, it was cool, what's cooking?'

Toby was cutting up vegetables. 'A few work colleagues are coming for drinks and lunch. We'll have it on the roof,' Aunt Jean said.

'How many people are coming?' I asked, looking at Toby.

'Oh, just four.'

'Do they know about us?' I asked.

'Not much other than you're my niece and nephew and you live with me.'

'Did you tell them what happened?' I was alarmed.

'No, not all the details. I told them your mother, little brother and sister were killed in tragic circumstances.'

'Should I put the olives next to the tomatoes, or the fetta?' Toby was absorbed. I wasn't even sure he heard our conversation.

'Mix them up,' Aunt Jean replied.

I kept looking at Toby. I'd never seen him helping Mum or me get food ready and he was obviously enjoying himself.

'Can I do anything to help?' I offered. Toby wasn't going to look at me, so I gave up staring at him.

'Get yourself breakfast, and then you can help me fill the eggs.'

I grabbed the cereal. I ate quietly, looking around

the kitchen. I love the colours Aunt Jean has painted it, the same colours as the beach, soft blues and yellows, it's so light. I love the little knick-knacks and the way the pots and pans hang above the stove. It all seemed so modern compared to the kitchen I'd grown up with. I finished my breakfast and took my bowl to the sink and washed it. There was already washing-up water in it, as Aunt Jean believed in washing-up as she cooked so there wasn't such a mess at the end.

'I'm ready, what can I do?'

Aunt Jean showed me how to fill the eggs from the anchovy mixture she'd made. I'd never done this before, in fact, I'd never had an anchovy till I'd come here to live. We'd always had the same thing, back on the farm, night after night, week after week. Roast lamb and vegetables on Sunday, cold left-over lamb and vegetables on Monday, lamb chops and vegetables Tuesday, lamb stew Wednesday. Dad killed a sheep every couple of months, and sometimes we'd have kangaroo or rabbit that he'd shot, but not often. On Fridays we would have fish and chips or Chinese take-away, because that was the day Mum did the shopping. Now here we eat all sorts of things, things I can't even pronounce. Toby and I had been too polite to say no to some of the strange food that Aunt Jean prepared or got from a take-away, and now the only lamb we mostly have is in a souvlaki. Aunt Jean doesn't eat much meat, but she said one day we could cook roast lamb. Toby wanted it, but Aunt Jean said to wait till winter. She said Toby and I could cook it, because it was important that we both learned to cook. Toby had carried on a bit until Aunt Jean said a lot of top chefs were male. I said I couldn't figure that out, when women did most of the cooking.

I wondered what Dad would say if he saw Toby standing there, with an apron on, cutting up vege-tables? I could hear him thunder at Toby, That's not a man's job, get that bloody apron off! At least Toby would grow up different to Dad, I thought. Dad would have also gone on about what he called chink food. I remember the first time Mum had brought Chinese home instead of the usual fish and chips, there'd almost been a riot. The food had ended up all over the walls and the floor as Dad had ranted on about Vietnam and communists. He said he'd never allow his children to be polluted by their ways and their food. It was because he'd been in Vietnam, fighting the Vietnamese and it had done something bad to his brain. He had a lot of hate in him and it was scary sometimes the way he'd lose it for no reason and go berserk. We'd gone to bed that night without any tea, leaving Mum and Dad yelling at each other and breaking plates and things. Why was I thinking about Dad? It must have been the newspaper. Maybe Dad was trying to get in my mind from his prison cell by focusing his mind on me. Some people believed that people could do that. I just wanted him out of my head. I concentrated on the eggs.

'What time do you expect your friends?' I asked Aunt Jean.

'About one-thirty.'

'Could we go for a swim?' Toby asked.

'Actually, I might come with you,' Aunt Jean said, as she sliced tomatoes.

'I might go later. I don't like it at this time of day, when it's so crowded,' I said.

'It's always crowded, I want to go,' said Toby.

'If anyone arrives, tell them I won't be long,' Aunt Jean said to me.

They left. I thought that I better try and write a letter to Ruby. It would be good if she got it before she arrived in a few days. I got out the writing pad that I'd got for my twelfth birthday. I like hand-writing letters sometimes. I mean, I know you can write heaps on the computer, but what if you forgot how to write and the world ran out of electricity. You'd spent all your years using a keyboard and you forgot how to actually write with a pen. Well, these

49

things could happen. I remember how Grandma Collins would go on about not believing the changes in her lifetime whenever she visited the farm, not that she visited often, she'd shake her head and say, Can't believe it, over and over again. It's the only thing I remember about her.

I stared out the window. A butterfly was flapping its way upward. Who'd believe a butterfly would be able to find its way to a rooftop garden? We stared at each other. Well, I mean it seemed to look me in the eyes as it passed by. Wow, I thought. It's so fragile and beautiful with its pattern of red and black curved stripes and distinct white spots. Going where the wind blew and then getting back on to the track it was pursuing. It disappeared above the rooftop.

I couldn't seem to get past 'Dear Ruby'. I chewed on the pen. I love getting letters, why is it so hard to write them? I creased up my face thinking what could I say that would be interesting? Sometimes I feel like I don't know who I am or if I have anything to say. Which Jules was the real me? The one that Aunt Jean saw? The one my friends saw? Was I crazy? I knew I had to try and think positive things about myself, but I just felt so sad, I didn't have the energy. Bad thoughts seemed easier. You didn't have to think about them; they'd just come. If I tried to think of something good about myself it hurt my brain.

I thought about the party again. I suppose I sort of had a good time. Jasmine, Phoebe and I laughed heaps and I met a couple of other great people. The music was pretty cool and there was nice food. But then there was the other part, the alcohol and everything. Out-of-it people can be pretty ugly. I'm glad I was told not to drink the fruit punch. Jasmine told me that some girls that didn't know, got raped, or even bashed. I was horrified. I swore then and there to always take my own drink to a party. Water, Jasmine said, was the only thing you could taste something else in. What would Ruby think about all this? I reckon she'd say it was dangerous. I'd tell her in person, and just write a quick letter telling her how I couldn't wait to see her.

The phone rang. I ignored it and left it to answer itself and kept writing. I hadn't heard Aunt Jean or Toby get back, but that didn't mean they hadn't. Gee, I thought, I could be one of those people who were robbed while they were at home and never heard a thing. I froze and could only hear traffic noises. I didn't expect burglars to be making a lot of noise. Maybe I couldn't hear them because they were cat burglars, you know, the silent ones. I better have a look. I opened my bedroom door slowly, and peeked down the hall. I couldn't see anyone. I tiptoed quickly along to Toby's room and got his cricket bat. I put my head around the wall to the lounge room. Nothing. I entered the empty kitchen.

Part of me knew I was being ridiculous, this place was a fortress. Aunt Jean said she dared any punk to try breaking in. Deadlocks, alarms; only people with keys or who were buzzed up got into this building. I waited for a moment. Nothing. I was glad no one could see me scared like this, but better safe than sorry. I opened the fridge door.

There was a buzz from the intercom and I nearly hit the roof I jumped so high. It buzzed again and I pressed the intercom.

'Hi, Jean, it's us.'

'Um, she's not here, are you her friends?' They answered yes and said she expected them. I pressed the button that unlocked the building's front doors. I waited at our door looking through the peephole. There were three women and a man. They looked sort of harmless so I let them in.

'You must be Julie,' a woman said. 'I'm Diane, this is Rose, Wendy and Paul.' They all shook my hand.

'Hi,' I said. They all had bottles of wine and beer. More alcohol, I thought.

'Smells good,' said Rose appreciatively.

'Aunt Jean is at the beach, she won't be long,' I said quietly, feeling shy. I hadn't met many of Aunt Jean's friends and these were people she worked with and I think they're lawyers like Aunt Jean.

Each of them seemed familiar with the apartment as they put wine and beer in the fridge. Wendy put the kettle on and Paul started reading the paper open on the table.

'God I hate this newspaper,' Paul said suddenly.

'Well don't read it,' Rose replied.

'All the advertising. Pages and pages of full-page ads,' Paul continued, 'where's the bloody real news?'

'There are some good journalists,' Diane added.

'Who wants a coffee?' Wendy asked brightly.

They all said yes, and I didn't know what to do with myself. I hoped Paul didn't notice Dad's picture. I thought I could just sneak off to my room. The front door opened and Aunt Jean and Toby came in.

'Hi everyone! Toby, this is Diane, Paul, Rose and Wendy. I'll just have a quick shower to wash the salt off. Won't be a minute.' Aunt Jean left the room and I could hear the water running. Toby had gone straight to his room after he'd shaken everyone's hand. I was standing there like a dead duck. I didn't have anything to say to them and they seemed to have forgotten I was there. I started walking towards my room when Aunt Jean came out of the bathroom.

'Julie, can you help me take the food to the roof? Toby!' she called. 'Shower is free.'

The party on the roof was pretty loud for so few people, I thought. They popped champagne corks. Aunt Jean put her foot down about Toby and Paul aiming at people in the street. Toby and I even had a small glass of champagne. I hoped I didn't become an alcoholic from a glass. Was it like that? Once you tasted it you wanted more? I hoped not. People said it was like that with cigarettes. One puff and you were addicted. I nearly said no, like they said at my old school to say if anyone offers you drugs, just say no. They said they were all drugs, alcohol, cigarettes, and even tea and coffee. Surely Aunt Jean doesn't want me to become an alcoholic. She wouldn't offer me a drink. Of course she wouldn't. It was quite bubbly and sour. Weird. I couldn't imagine myself getting hooked on this stuff. I felt a bit silly though and even giggled a bit.

I watched Toby. He was acting like a wine waiter. Opening bottles and pouring like he was born to it. I hoped he wouldn't become an alcoholic either. There was a slight breeze off the sea and it felt cool on my face. An umbrella had been set up and we sat in its shade. The sun beat down relentlessly.

'Do you know why they call this Ben Buckler?' Paul indicated the cliff tops with his arm.

'There are several theories,' Aunt Jean answered, 'I don't think anyone really knows which one is true.'

'What are they?' asked Rose.

'Well, one is that it was named after Ben Buckler, an escaped convict who lived with the Aborigines of La Perouse for ten years. He was killed by the collapsing of the shelf rock he was standing on, somewhere there.' Aunt Jean pointed towards the cliff edge to our left. 'I think it was about 1820.'

We all looked over the edge. 'Is that when you were born?' I asked innocently.

'Some things don't change,' Diane laughed. 'Remember how we used to say the same thing to our mother when we were teenagers?'

They all laughed, but not me. Aunt Jean wasn't my mother. I looked at Toby and he looked like thunder. I gave him the look that said, Don't say anything. None of the adults noticed.

'Then there is the Aboriginal word, "Baal-buckaler" that some believe became Ben Buckler.'

'That's the one I believe,' Paul said.

'Did you know Coogee supposedly means stinky?' Rose asked.

Everyone laughed. 'I didn't know that,' Aunt Jean said.

I got over my anger because I was interested in the conversation, I don't think Diane meant to be mean. I looked out to the cliffs and then up the road to where the lagoons had been. I'd read somewhere that Aborigines used to catch ducks on the lagoons that went from the beach to what is now tiled rooftops all the way to Rose Bay. I thought about the name Bondi. It had come from the word the Aborigines called this place, 'Boondi' which means 'water breaking over rocks'. They were gone now, the tribe, the language and the only signs they'd ever been here were rock carvings around the heads. I wondered if anywhere in the whole of NSW there were descendants of the Bondi tribe, left? I'd ask Ruby when she got here, she might know.

'It sure looks like they're making a mess down there.' Diane pointed to the southern end of the beach where a huge fence stretched across the sand. It was where they were building the Olympic beach volleyball venue.

'It's been a total schamozzle,' Aunt Jean said.

'I've read about it,' Paul said, 'but I didn't realise how bad it was till I saw it when we came down Bondi Road.'

'Most of the residents are very unhappy about it, but every objection that was brought up fell on deaf ears, a bit like the railway station they're planning for the southern end of the park.'

'It seems some people won't be happy till Bondi looks like the Gold Coast.' Rose said. 'You'll have to move Jean.'

Move, I thought, no way, I like it here.

'My family's been in Bondi for generations, they won't be getting rid of me,' laughed Aunt Jean. I was glad to hear that. 'Everyone is hoping that the winter tides will wash any structure they build for the Olympics into the sea.'

They all had an opinion and talked over the top of each other. I was glad when they stopped, it's all you ever heard at the shops, even the beach, and Aunt Jean sure moaned on about it a lot. Toby pretended to cover a yawn when I looked at him and it made me laugh.

I helped gather up some of the plates and followed Aunt Jean into the kitchen. Wendy had gone to the toilet.

'Are you alcoholics?' I was upset that they were drinking so much.

'Oh dear, Julie.' She looked at me. 'Not everyone who drinks alcohol is an alcoholic. I don't consider myself one, but I can't vouch for my friends. It is a very complicated issue. I'd like to sit down and talk about it with you sometime, but not now.' She pushed my hair back from my face. 'Maybe tonight, how about that? Are you all right?'

I nodded, turning away from her gaze.

The phone rang; I raced to answer it to get away. It was Phoebe and we talked for hours about the party and I laughed so much I nearly wet myself. It felt like after talking to Phoebe that I'd got something over with, almost like a kind of initiation into their world. Maybe I hadn't had such a bad time really. I knew I wouldn't say anything to Aunt Jean about the drinking and stuff, I mean it was just a normal teenage party, after all, nothing for her to worry about, it wasn't her that went to them.

CHAPTER 5

Sunday Night

Everyone had gone by the time I got off the phone. I'd heard them all shout goodbye but I didn't answer. Aunt Jean suggested we take the leftovers and have a picnic on the beach. It had emptied a lot by about seven and most of the family groups had gone from the beach. Toby made me laugh when he said he thought city people were more disobedient than sheep, even though they all flocked together.

I raced in and dived under the waves. It was fantastic, I then swam out and waited for a wave to body-surf. Toby joined me and as the right wave came, we both started kicking, desperate to catch it properly. It picked me up and I zoomed along with my hands clenched together in front of me. Wow, I got nearly to shore without being dumped. Toby hadn't ridden it as well as me. I saw him a little way out, bobbing up and down; I swam out to him.

'Did you see that?' I asked him excitedly. 'It was wicked.'

'I don't know why I missed it, I thought I started kicking at the right time.'

'Let's see if we can catch the next one.'

We surfed in and swam out hundreds of times, and had figured out that if we waited for every third or fourth wave that they'd be the best ones. I finally felt exhausted and made my way to where Aunt Jean was reading a book on the sand.

'Did you see us?' I asked her.

'Some of the time, you both seem to have got the hang of body-surfing.'

'I can't wait to get a board, I'm going to start saving up,' I said, staring out at the continual waves.

'Maybe we could enrol you in surfing lessons that they have here in the summer.'

'That'd be great.' I was excited and couldn't wait.

'Are you hungry?' Aunt Jean asked.

'You bet,' said Toby as he sank to his knees in the sand.

We ate in silence as the light was changing in the sky and the last of the day was near. We started packing up as the sky grew dark.

'Would you like an ice cream?' Aunt Jean asked. We both nodded our heads.

'It is a pity I have to work tomorrow,' Aunt Jean said, as we crossed the road.

Campbell Parade has millions of take-away shops and most of them had a few people in them. The nightlife was just beginning, with a different crowd coming out at sundown. A lot of the people looked a bit desperate if you ask me, and I avoided eye contact with any of them. All the shops had heaps of lights on so the street was as light as day. The fast-food everywhere made the street smell of cooked meat, fish and chips and coffee. Rubbish bins were overflowing, yet people still kept putting their rubbish on top; I suppose they were doing the right thing.

We passed a man holding out a cup, asking for money to feed his family. He had a sign saying he was a refugee from Albania or somewhere, and Aunt Jean gave him money and our leftover food.

'Why did you do that?' Toby asked. 'Costas at school, says all reffos should be sent back,' Toby said.

Aunt Jean and I looked at each other. 'Oh dear,' Aunt Jean said.

'Toby,' I said, 'how come Costas says that, and how come you believe him?'

'Costas is cool. What's a reffo anyway?' Toby asked.

'Toby, I'd prefer you not to use the word "reffo" around me.' Aunt Jean's voice stung, even I felt it.

61

'Your family and probably Costas' have had members who've come to Australia as what you call reffos.'

'It's not my fault, that's what everyone calls them at school, I didn't know reffos were refugees, I thought they were boat people or something, why are you always picking on me, why don't you ever pick on Julie?' Toby spat out and started running up the street.

'Toby!' I shouted. He didn't stop. 'Toby!' I yelled even louder, he stopped.

Aunt Jean and I caught up to him. 'I'm not saying it's your fault, Toby.' Aunt Jean grabbed his arm. 'I know it's sometimes hard to disagree with your mates, but I think you ought to think about what they're saying and what you can find out for yourself by asking the right questions.'

Toby looked puzzled. 'Whatever,' he said shaking her hand off his arm.

'Toby, refugees are people who have to flee real horror we can't even imagine. Here we worry about what sort of wine to buy with dinner. I don't want to go on about it, but these people are real, Toby. Why do you think we shouldn't help them? Why should we send them back to a country that might murder them because a part of their ankle was seen, or where bombs are still raining down on houses and hospitals? Why, when we've got all this,' Aunt Jean waved her arms around, 'why should we do that?'

Aunt Jean was very angry and I wished that this whole thing had never started, especially in the street. I looked at Toby and knew he was thinking about it.

'Let's get the ice creams, I'm having double choc-chipped chocolate,' I said and raced into the ice cream bar.

No more was said in the shop or as we walked along licking our ice creams. We crossed the road to Bondi Park, and walked past the Pavilion, which was all lit up. I could hear Spanish music coming from the upstairs window. As we walked past the arches there was the hum of lots of voices talking in the various restaurants and take-aways. There were also people walking or sitting on the grass in groups or pairs, chattering, eating and kissing and stuff. I tried not to look, so I looked at the beach, where people were in the dark water. The lights from the promenade reflected back from the beach. I haven't swum at night yet; I wondered if sharks swam at night or went to sleep?

We reached the flat. 'I'll tell you both sometime about some of your relations who were refugees, but not tonight,' Aunt Jean said as we got inside.

I had the first shower, and even though I loved the sea, I loved washing the salt out of my stiff hair. As I dried myself, I thought about how Aunt Jean's views were so different to Dad's, but probably more like Mum's. I felt sad when Mum came in to my mind, I missed her so much and I miss my little brother and sister, even though sometimes they'd annoyed me. I couldn't bear thinking about my dead dog, Jesse. I picked my bathers up out of the shower and gave them another rinse under the tap. Did you like living here, Mum, did you love the beach? I wondered as I wrung the last drops of water out.

I picked up my toothbrush and looked in the mirror. Why did you let us grow up living on a sheep farm in the middle of nowhere? How come you never brought us here? I asked Mum, staring at myself, wishing for an answer. I noticed my eyes didn't seem so far apart today, they looked sad. Was there such a thing as sad-looking eyes, or is it just me who thinks that's how mine look? Questions, questions but where were the answers? I wondered if Mum would have known any answers to things that bothered me? I was determined I wasn't going to cry and fought the tears till my eyes stung. I had to stop with this crying business, I was sick of the never-ending supply of tears I seemed to have. Please help me Mum, I whispered to the mirror. If you can't answer my questions at least help me stop crying. Where have you gone Mum, where are you? I rubbed my face and gargled some water. Mirror, mirror on the wall, why's life such a stuff up? I said and turned my back and took a deep breath.

When I came out of the bathroom, Toby and Aunt Jean were playing backgammon. I was a bit surprised considering what had happened in the street. I put on my nothing-is-bothering-me face and looked over their shoulders.

'You can play the winner, if you'd like?' Aunt Jean said.

'Sure.' I picked up a magazine. I was glad Toby seemed better, maybe they'd talked a bit while I was in the shower. Aunt Jean would have asked Toby if he wanted a game while they waited for the shower. Toby wouldn't have been able to resist because he loved games, like chess and things. They'd rung Mrs Thompson and she'd said Toby could definitely come and stay for some of the holidays, and that would have cheered him up as well.

'I'm not sure what you two would like to do for the next few days?' Aunt Jean looked up. 'Have you any ideas?'

'The movies,' Toby said, 'and skateboarding.'

'The movies, looking in the shops, and surfing,' I said.

Aunt Jean looked worried. 'I wish I could take tomorrow off, but it's completely impossible, I'm afraid,' she sighed.

'We'll be right,' I said.

Since we'd moved here, apart from the beach and catching the bus to school, we'd gone everywhere with Aunt Jean. I'd been amazed the first time we'd caught a bus into the city; it was so crowded with tall buildings. I got a sore neck from looking up, and hoped they wouldn't fall over, because some of them sure looked like they were leaning towards the street. I caught a lot of flies that day, walking around with my mouth open. I couldn't believe all the different shops with so many different things that you never even imagined existed. My favourite was this little chocolate shop that sold these amazing shaped chocolates that are too delicious to describe.

I also loved Circular Quay with all the ferries lining up looking important. It's great watching them come into berth and wondering if they are going to crash into the pier or not, some seem to come in so fast. I've caught them to Manly, Balmain and Hunters Hill. I stood up the front where the waves spray you, and imagined I was the captain. A couple of times tourists had asked me to take their photo with the Harbour Bridge or Opera House in the background. I always hoped they turned out the best ones of their holiday and make them think of the girl with sad eyes on the ferry. Aunt Jean said she would take us to Taronga Zoo sometime. I suppose it's not a cool thing for a fifteen-year old to do, but I really want to see some of the animals that I've only ever seen pictures of, like rhinoceros and gorillas. Maybe Ruby and I could go on our own when she comes to stay, that'd be better than going with Aunt Jean.

The sound of the backgammon counters clicked. 'Where did you move, Toby?' Aunt Jean asked, and he showed her. 'Good move.'

'Jasmine and Phoebe said I could go shopping with them, maybe Tuesday.'

'Have you saved any pocket money, either of you?'

We both nodded. I remembered when Aunt Jean had asked us how much pocket money we used to get, and we told her, none, because there never was enough money, even though Mum had tried sometimes to give us some. Usually she'd have to borrow it back again. Aunt Jean asked some of her friends and I asked Jasmine and Phoebe and we agreed on a sum. Toby and I both had to do our share of the housework though. I was better trained than Toby. I realised now how much housework

Mum and I'd done, and how little Dad and Toby had done. I mean Toby used to do the washing-up with me, but he never folded clothes or ironed or vacuumed. You should have seen his face the first time he ironed. I'd laughed for hours because he'd looked so shocked.

One day, last week, Toby and I had a big argument. Toby had said he didn't like Aunt Jean and the way she made him do girl things. I got angry and attacked him with the feather duster, asking him how doing your own washing or ironing, or making your own school lunch, could be seen as a girl thing? He said none of his friends made their lunch, washed their clothes, none of them even washed-up! He said no way could he invite his friends here, because Aunt Jean would probably make him do the ironing or something and then he wouldn't have any friends. I got nowhere with him that day, so I just let him cool off. We hadn't talked about it again, but I knew we would. I didn't want Toby hating Aunt Jean because she wasn't Mum; he shouldn't take that out on her. He seemed okay today though, when he and Aunt Jean were preparing lunch. Maybe he'd got over it, we both seemed to go up and down lots, like yo-yos. I sighed quietly and went back to the magazine.

'Gee, this is shit!'

'Julie!'

'Sorry, but it is.'

'What is?'

'What's on bloody TV.' I looked at the television program with disgust.

'Julie, swearing sounds awful.' Aunt Jean looked at me.

'Everyone does it,' I replied defensively.

'I know everyone does, but it's good to not let it become a habit.'

'Sure.' I really meant, Shut up.

'There are appropriate places and inappropriate places. It's a good idea to remember that. You too, Toby.' She looked at him.

'What did I do?'

'Nothing, I'm just asking you to listen.'

'Whatever,' he answered.

Aunt Jean knew when to not push. 'A drop of rain can become a flood,' she once said. Somehow it was like Toby and I would send up this wall around us and nobody was going to get on our side. I could feel it, a barrier, repelling all aliens.

Toby won the backgammon and we set up while Aunt Jean went off to get her work stuff ready.

'You have to bare your bum if I backgammon you,' I said, challenging him.

'Crap! *No way!*'

It was silent except for the rolling of the dice and the click of the counters. This is how we played, concentrating quietly. We'd only learnt the game since we'd been living here. Aunt Jean said we were both good learners, but I reckon sometimes she'd let us win.

Toby won the first game, but I reckon it was because he'd had the practice of the games with Aunt Jean. We set up again.

'Gee, holidays are different here, aren't they?' Toby said, as I threw the dice.

'Yeah, even though they just started.'

'It didn't used to matter what we did. We could do anything.'

'Yeah, but there was nothing to do, remember?'

Aunt Jean came back into the room. 'I've got to leave early in the morning. How about you catch the bus and meet me at lunchtime at work? Pick out a movie and we'll go from there.'

'What time should we catch the bus?'

'Look up the timetable yourselves, it's in the bottom draw.'

Toby and I looked at each other. 'I'll get it,' he said.

'I'll leave your fares on the bench. Goodnight.'

'Goodnight,' we both replied.

When Aunt Jean had closed the door, Toby said. 'Remember when Mum used to say, Sweet dreams?'

My throat sort of swelled and I thought I was going to cry. 'Yeah,' I finally said.

'I miss that,' he said, looking as sad as I felt.

'Which movie do you want to see?' I asked, changing the subject.

'Don't know what's on.'

'We'll look in the paper after this game.'

We continued playing till, eventually, I won a very close game. Neither of us said anything more about Mum.

'Best of three?' Toby asked.

'No, I want an early night.'

'Oh, go on,' he whined.

'No, let's look at the paper.' I opened to the movie section. There were so many bloody movies.

'How about this one,' Toby said pointing to the last one I'd ever want to see.

'No. Too violent.'

'What about this one?'

'Too stupid.'

'Well which one then?'

'How about this one,' I said pointing to my choice.

'What's it about?'

'It's about this girl . . .'

'Not a girl movie,' he interrupted.

'And this boy,' I continued, ignoring him.

71

'Not a mushy one where they're kissing all the time. Yuk, yuk, yuk.'

'Toby shut up. I'm not going to tell you anything else, except they're surfers.'

'Surfers?'

'Yep.'

'You're making that up.'

'Why would I lie?'

'I don't know, but you would.'

'I'm not. It's got great music and even if there is a bit of kissing, it won't be much. It's mostly about the ocean.'

'I hate kissing movies.'

'One day you won't. You'll be kissing someone yourself.'

'Never,' he said adamantly.

'Everybody does.'

'Well not me, no way, never ever.'

I wished I had a tape recorder so that I could play this conversation back to him when he was older.

'Would you write it down and sign it,' I said.

'What?'

'I'd like it in writing.'

'Why?' Toby asked suspiciously.

'Because one day I'll be able to wave it in your face and say, Never say never.'

'Okay.'

72

I got a pad out of the drawer. 'I'll tell you what to write.'

'You're the boss.'

'I will never kiss anyone in my life, except relatives.' Toby wrote as I dictated, and signed it with a flourish. 'Where are you going to keep it?' he asked.

'Somewhere safe.' I folded it up, carefully. 'Somewhere secret.' I put it in my pocket.

'Maybe we could go for a swim in the morning before we catch the bus.' Toby said, hopefully.

'I don't know.'

'Why did this happen to us?' he asked, looking out the window.

I knew what he meant. 'I don't know,' I replied. 'I just don't know.'

We both were silent, staring out the window. You could see the lights of a ship on the horizon, making slow progress. The cliffs were dotted with suburban lights, in some places right to the edge. The moon was nearly full, high in the eastern sky. I yawned. 'Let's figure it out in the morning.'

As my head hit the pillow, I fell asleep almost instantly. Maybe it's the sea air.

CHAPTER 6

Monday Morning

I wandered into the kitchen just as Aunt Jean was finishing her breakfast.

'Good morning,' I said, yawning.

'Good morning, Julie,' Aunt Jean replied, as she sipped her coffee, 'I'd have thought you would sleep in this morning.'

'Couldn't,' I said, truthfully, 'must be still tuned into school time.'

'I'm in a rush. Could you and Toby meet me at twelve-thirty at my office?'

'Sure.'

'You remember how to get there?'

'Sure, I remember from that last time we caught the bus.'

'I must say that you both are good at remembering landmarks.' Aunt Jean smiled at me. 'You must have learnt that in the bush.'

'Toby and I used to go for long walks, looking for treasure. We never got lost.'

'Did you find treasure?'

'Well, not really. We were looking for gold.'

Aunt Jean laughed, 'God, look at the time, I'll have to take the car.'

Aunt Jean believed in public transport even though most of the time she missed the bus. It didn't stop her from trying each day to be early enough to catch it. I didn't know if, since we'd been here, she'd missed it more often.

I got the cereal and a bowl out of the cupboard. Aunt Jean called out goodbye as she flew out the door. The street had the busy sound of a working day and I could smell the bakery. This was one of those things that I had never imagined I'd find so comforting. The fresh-cooked-bread and pastry smell was so new to me, I felt I could almost taste the fresh bread. On the farm, the only thing I'd smelt was sheep. I'd written about the bread smell to Ruby in one of my first letters and couldn't wait till she came and smelt it herself; it was only a couple of days now.

Toby wandered in, looking more asleep than awake. He went straight to the breakfast things, then to the fridge and sat down at the table. You'd almost think he was sleep walking, he didn't say a word and I wasn't sure that he even noticed me sitting there.

'Are you awake?'

'What?'

'Are you awake? You sure don't look it.'

'Course I'm awake, you idiot.'

'Well, good morning to you.'

'What?'

'Oh, forget it. Manners don't hurt, that's what Mum used to say.'

'Well she's dead, so who gives a stuff about manners?'

'*Toby.*'

'Well, it's true,' he said, defying me to try and get out of that.

'Just because Mum is dead,' I said, quietly, 'doesn't mean manners are.'

'Oh, whatever.' He went back to eating his breakfast.

I didn't want to continue. Something about the way Toby had said Mum was dead, jarred me. It was the way he said it, like he didn't care any more, but I knew that wasn't true, he'd talked about missing her last night. He cried about her, I knew. He still hated Dad. I caught him one day crying over a photograph Aunt Jean had of all of us. He'd taken the photo out of the frame and had cut Dad out of it. He'd cut Dad's face up in tiny pieces and threw them off the balcony.

'Aunt Jean said to meet her at her office at twelve-thirty.' I broke the silence between us.

'What time is it?'

'Look at the bloody clock yourself.'

He did and seemed to calm down a bit. 'I don't think I'll go for a swim.'

'We'll have to catch a bus about half-past, quarter-to.' I looked at him. 'What is your problem?'

'Sometimes I think Aunt Jean doesn't like me because I am a boy. You know how she says men stink, well what does she think I am?'

'Well you certainly aren't a man,' I said. 'It's just an expression, she doesn't mean you, lots of women say it but they don't necessarily mean every man.'

'She's always yelling at me to put the toilet seat down. How am I meant to remember every time? Mum didn't go on about it.'

'Toby, it annoys me too, Mum just gave up. It drives me crazy every time I go to the toilet and the seat is up!'

'It annoys me every time I go and the seat's down, so what, do I go on about it? Why is it such a big deal with you chicks?'

'Toby, how many times do I have to tell you, we aren't chicks?'

He mumbled something. 'What did you say?' I demanded.

'Nothing.'

'I'll twist your ears back if you don't tell me what you said.' I moved towards him menacingly.

My hands became crab pincers, opening and shutting. He took off, ran out of the room and slammed his door.

'You're a fairy, you're a fairy.' He called from behind the closed barricaded door.

This was what the boys at school called other boys when they were being abusive; it certainly wasn't what we said to be insulting in the country. I mean weren't fairies meant to be good things and it was the elves and goblins that were bad, so why didn't they call each other goblin or something? I couldn't figure them out.

'Open this door, Toby or you're going to be very sorry.' I pushed against it. While he felt safe he could say anything he liked and he kept on with his stupid fairy refrain.

'What are you going on about, you dickhead?' I pushed but he was quite strong and I could only make the door budge a little. 'This is childish,' I said, giving up and walking back to the kitchen. What was his problem? I looked at the clock. We had an hour till the bus. Toby was like a hot and cold tap. Last night he seemed fine, playing backgammon with Aunt Jean. This morning, he'd changed into the hormone kid again.

I went and got my letter-writing things. I would finish my letter to Ruby and post it on my way to

78

the bus. I started writing. I heard Toby open his door. I could tell he was sneaking down the hall to see what I was doing. I kept writing. I knew he was looking at me. I ignored him.

'You're a fairy,' he shouted and ran down the hall back to his room.

How childish! How absolutely pathetic! I wrote about it to Ruby. She'd laugh with me, I was sure. What do you do with a brother who is going off his head?

Toby must have realised that I wasn't going to chase him, because I heard his door again. I wanted to grab him and flush his head down the toilet, but I knew it was only fantasy. We hadn't ever fought physically, except mucking around, before we moved here. I didn't want to fight with him. I was stronger than he was, it wasn't that. I just didn't want to hurt anyone like I'd been hurt when Mum or Dad had hit me. I suppose you could say I had a phobia about pain. It wasn't just receiving it, but giving it too. Was there something wrong with me, that I didn't enjoy being belted and didn't like belting anyone?

I put the pen down. I remembered how in grade six I had to fight with Tina Evans. It was a pride thing and before I knew, it had become the main bout of the year for all the school. Word had spread like wildfire about the big fight behind the shelter shed. Toby told me he was going to sell hot dogs. The fight was set for lunchtime, Friday. The closer it got the more I felt sick. I wanted to stay home from school, but knew that then everyone would say I was a coward, even if I had a brain tumour or something. Even remembering it now, made me squirm.

I got up and put the kettle on. I could hear music from Toby's room. That was good. It would calm him down. Didn't they say music calmed the savage beast or something?

I'd wished Tina Evans had been calmed down by music, she'd come punching at me and hit me fair in the mouth. I wasn't even ready and Toby had asked me later if I expected to hear a bell to start the fight. I was shocked at the hatred behind the punch. I knew I had to save face and hit her back. The punch crunched right into her cheekbone. She got a shock, I got a shock. Someone yelled out, teachers, and everyone ran except Tina and me. We just stared at each other. I tried not to cry even though my eyes were stinging with tears. I could see a big mark on her face, and I tasted blood in my mouth. It was horrible. We were caught, but Tina got most of the blame; she had a reputation as a fighter. We had to pick up all the papers in the whole of the school. It wasn't too bad, we got out of class for the afternoon. As we walked around we sort of became friends. I shuddered even now, thinking of the feel of punching someone. I didn't think I would ever forget it, and I knew I never wanted to do it again.

I'd be hopeless defending myself, I suddenly thought. If anyone attacked me, I'd just go to pieces. Maybe I just better never go out anywhere, I thought, glumly. Never leave the flat; no one would miss me. I'll just stare out the window and grow really old like Aunt Jean. I could do school by correspondence, but why would I bother when I was never going to go out. I knew I was being stupid, but it had never stopped me before from thinking the worst. The phone rang.

'Hello.'

'Julie.'

'Yes.'

It was Aunt Jean. 'I've just got out of court. I haven't had a moment to ring, but listen.'

I swallowed hard. I had a strong feeling something was wrong. I answered warily.

'What's up?'

'Have you seen the morning paper?'

'No, I haven't been out.'

'Oh dear, oh well, your father has somehow managed to get a sob story in about wanting to see his children. Some of the things are almost libellous.'

'He hasn't?' I was shocked. All my bad feelings about Dad over the weekend were now making sense.

'I'm afraid so Julie. I thought I'd better warn you so you didn't get a paper to look up the movies.'

'We decided last night,' I said quietly, trying to take in what Aunt Jean had said. 'When will it end?' I felt like crying again. Why couldn't Dad understand we didn't want to have anything to do with him? Was he so stupid or what? What did he expect? Toby and me to hug him and say we forgive him for killing our mother, brother, sister and dog? Burning our house down? I wished he'd just get real and forget us, because sure as hell I wanted to forget him. I wasn't religious, but now I prayed to the sky for peace, for me and Toby and every other kid who lived in hell. I didn't wish horrible things for my Dad, I just didn't think about him and whenever he came into my mind I chased him out by humming or whatever it took. I must still sort of love him in some weird way because it hurt if I thought about him and what he'd done. I hated him also, for taking our family and our life away; I was so confused, how can you love someone who you hate? His lawyer told Aunt Jean that Dad wanted to say sorry to Toby and I. Somehow I don't think it would be enough.

'Are you there Julie? Don't let this ruin your day. The rag that published this crap is in for it, don't you worry.'

I could see Aunt Jean standing there with that serious look that Mum, her and I seemed to share. 'Oh Aunt Jean, I'm just sick of it,' I paused. 'Is it safe to get the bus?'

'You'll be right, they haven't printed his name or photo, if you get the eleven-forty-six, you'll be right. Just leave in time to catch the bus, remember he's locked up in jail and can't get you.'

Was a day going to come when I would have to see my father again? I felt sick at the thought of it happening. I could imagine all sorts of reactions, but would never know what I'd do till it happened, and I never wanted it to happen, believe me. I also didn't want to feel sorry for him, even though they said he was mentally sick. No sane man could have done what he did. They called it Post Traumatic Stress Syndrome from his time in Vietnam as a soldier when he was nineteen. There wasn't any counselling or anything when he got back, he was meant to just get on with life as if the horrific experiences of war could just be forgotten. Mum used to say we couldn't possibly dream the horrors our father went through. I knew he'd been trained to kill as a soldier, but killing his own family? I just

83

couldn't understand it. My stomach knotted at the thought of looking in to his eyes. I wondered if they were still bloodshot?

'Julie, Julie.' Aunt Jean's voice seemed to come from along way away.

'Sorry, I just can't believe it.' Tears fell from my eyes and I tasted their saltiness at the corner of my mouth. I licked it away.

'I'm angry, very angry, don't you worry, I'll take care of it,' Aunt Jean said quickly. 'I'm sorry, I've got to go.' I heard someone calling her in the background. 'Will you be all right? Do you still want to come and meet me?'

I thought for a moment about staying in my fortress. I almost laughed. I'd been plotting never leaving the flat again. I felt angry with Dad. Angry that he could ruin my day, angry that he could stop Toby and I from enjoying ourselves at a movie. I clenched my fist.

'He isn't going to stop us from going out. No way.' My tears were replaced with a steely calm. I'm going to enjoy myself, I thought. Go out and have a good time and forget about Dad.

'Good. Don't let him get to you,' Aunt Jean said firmly, 'I've really got to go, bye.'

'See you at half-past.' I hung up. I thought I'd better tell Toby the bad news. How was he meant to get better in the head, when he had to deal with what our father had done? Sometimes I thought it was harder for him because he was male. He wondered if it was genetic, the violence and the alcoholism. It scared him and he vowed he would never marry, nor have children, just in case. Aunt Jean tried to reassure him that you do make choices about how you behave. Anyone may have a violent streak, but it didn't mean they acted on it. That was the difference. I know sometimes, when Toby was in a particularly grumpy mood and nothing could be right, it was because he was afraid of his destiny. I tried to give him the example that there was no reason on earth why he should grow up like Dad, just like I wouldn't grow up to be like Mum. We were individuals, I told him, unique. We were the only one of us. Sometimes he seemed happy to believe it. Other times, he just brooded. I was happy when he was, unhappy when he was. I'd tell him later about the article in the paper, or maybe, never.

CHAPTER 7

Monday Afternoon

Toby and I were the only ones at the bus stop. I wouldn't let him go and buy anything at the shop. I told him it was because he might miss the bus, but really it's because I didn't want him to see a newspaper. The 360 bus came and there weren't that many people on it. We sat in the seat next to the back door. I stared at the huge Catholic schools we passed, along Blair Street, one was called O'Sullivan's and I wondered why. I thought schools look really different when they're empty, sort of spooky and lifeless.

'Would you like to go to that boy's school?' I pointed at the Christian Brothers School.

'Are you insane?'

I looked at my palms. 'I don't think so, I haven't got hairs growing on my palms.'

'That's cause you shaved them off.'

'Very funny, so funny, that must be why you spend so much time in the bathroom, shaving your palms, you know all about it.'

'No, I only shave my ears.'

'Toby, you're an idiot.'

He gave me one of his moronic looks. The bus was taking forever; we were only at Rose Bay. It was because all these people got on one stop and got off at the next. If I were the bus driver, I would have asked them why they didn't bloody well walk! More and more people got on as we headed down New South Head Road. They obviously decided to leave the Wales out of the road name because it would have sounded even more stupid than it does now. At last we pulled into Eddy Avenue.

'I thought it was only meant to be twenty minutes from Bondi,' I said as we got off, hoping the driver heard me.

'It is if you don't go through all the posh places,' Toby answered. 'Maybe next time we ought to catch the one that goes up Bondi Road.'

'Or get a train to Bondi Junction and then the bus.'

'Will we walk or get another bus or maybe even a train?'

'So much choice.' I put my hand on my forehead, 'Why don't we get a train to Circular Quay and walk from there?'

'Yeah, that'll be the quickest.'

We walked down the stairs from Broadway, along a tunnel decorated with paintings of scenes from all different countries, to the railway station. We bought tickets to the Quay from a machine and went through the turnstile. I couldn't get over how the trains went underground, under the city, with all those cars and buildings on top, and yet it didn't cave in. Amazing. I loved it when the train came out into the light of Circular Quay and in front of you was Sydney Cove. Looking down you could see ferries lined up, with people boarding or disembarking. There were little crowds gathered around the numerous buskers. We didn't have time to look at anything, so we walked quickly along Philip Street towards Aunt Jean's office.

We walked up the steps to the lobby. I looked around at the thick carpet and black furniture as we waited for Aunt Jean. There was this little alcove with a glass window and a light and rocks and plants with a waterfall. The sound of the trickling water made me feel like I wasn't in the middle of a city, but in the bush or something.

'Are you ready?' Aunt Jean came out of her office.

'Sure,' I said and Toby just nodded.

We had lunch in something called a brasserie and Toby kept on making jokes about bras and boobs. Even Aunt Jean got fed up and told him off. I could see the look on his face and it wasn't a good look.

I'd have to talk with him again. It didn't appear like my messages were getting through.

'When do you think Dad will go to court?' I asked quietly, looking around to make sure no one was listening. I caught Toby's eye and he gave me a sharp look.

'Probably June or July,' Aunt Jean answered.

'Have you heard anything about if we have to go?'

'Nothing definite. Your lawyers are trying to make sure, if you have to give evidence it will be done on video in a separate room, so you don't have to look at, or be intimidated by him.'

'But why would we have to give evidence?' Toby asked. 'We didn't see anything. We know he's guilty, guilty.' He banged his fist on the table each time he said guilty, like he was the judge or something. The cutlery jumped about, and I noticed a couple of people looking at us.

'Calm down,' I whispered to him.

'They'll want to know about your mother and father's relationship before . . .' Aunt Jean paused as if she were looking for the right words. There were no right words for my father's deed. None. 'Before your mother's death.'

'Before Mum was murdered,' Toby said, angrily.

'Yes, Toby. Before they were all murdered.' Aunt Jean looked defeated. It was like she was thinking how she was going to manage Toby's anger. Both our counsellors had suggested we have what they called emotional boxes. We bought these cheap little boxes from one of those $2 Stores. Toby put stickers over his saying, Beware, Danger, and things like that. I'd put, Keep Out, Private, on mine. We were meant to put all our bad thoughts and feelings in them by writing them on bits of paper. The counsellors said one day we'd just throw the boxes away; we'd know when we were ready, sort of when we felt safe again, I suppose. I don't know about Toby, but I used mine heaps. They were completely private and there's no way Toby and I would look in each other's, and I know Aunt Jean wouldn't dare.

Aunt Jean finally spoke, 'Toby, we all feel the same way you do, please don't be angry with me.'

I was shocked. Aunt Jean was crying, and in public too, how embarrassing. It was like she didn't care about all the other people in fancy suits seeing her. I looked around to see if anyone was looking at us, and a woman at the next table stared back at me. I could tell she had been listening. I poked my tongue out at her and then smiled angelically at her shocked face. It was enough to make her turn away.

Toby said, 'If they ask me anything, I'm going to tell the truth, the whole truth and nothing but the truth.'

'I hope so Toby, I hope so.' Aunt Jean's tears had stopped.

'Mum wasn't the only one Dad hit.' Toby said quietly.

'Did he hit you?' Aunt Jean asked.

Toby nodded and looked down at his plate and began moving the pasta around.

I was surprised Toby was telling Aunt Jean one of our secrets. Mum had made us swear we wouldn't tell anyone some of the things that went on and some of the punishments Dad dished out. It was our business and nobody else's. Why had Toby decided to say something now?

'What about you, Julie?'

'Sometimes, but he hit Toby and Mum more than me.' I started shredding my serviette. I stopped and looked at Aunt Jean. My eyes said, There's worse that you don't know, and her head shot back as if an arrow or something had hit her. She'd understood my silent message and was stunned into silence.

'What about Jonathon and Jennifer?' Aunt Jean finally asked in a much softer voice.

'Only normal, like to stop them crying, you know, or when one of them accidentally spilt milk or something,' I said shredding more of the serviette.

91

Aunt Jean was quiet. I looked at Toby. Why had he started this? I thought we'd agreed not to tell any adults about our family.

'Did your mother hit you?' Aunt Jean asked.

Toby and I looked at each other. Neither of us spoke.

'Did she?' Aunt Jean gently probed.

I decided I'd better answer. 'Sometimes, but she'd slap us, Dad would punch or use his belt, or a stick.'

'Mum sometimes used the wooden spoon,' Toby said.

I gave Toby my best shut-up-your-face look. He stared back icily. I'd often wondered if anyone would believe us if we ever told about Dad's punishments. I didn't think they would. Even as I thought of some, I found it hard to believe myself. It was all so far away, and sometimes I thought it was another Julie, not me, another one I seemed to hardly know.

'One day he hog-tied me. Do you know what I'd done wrong?' Toby asked.

'I can't imagine what you could have done to deserve such punishment,' Aunt Jean replied with a tremor in her voice. 'I can't imagine.'

I could tell she was trying not to cry. I looked at the waiters rushing in and out of the kitchen, willing myself not to crack up. My bottom lip trembled so I bit down on it to stop. I looked at Toby, wondering why he'd chosen this horrible story, wasn't it better if he just forgot about it? Toby took his time, as if he was travelling back to that day in his mind. I stared at him with my eyebrows raised. He started speaking and I turned away.

'I'd left a gate open in the wether's paddock and they got mixed up with some of the ewes and lambs,' he said disgustedly. 'Can you believe that? I was sure I'd shut the gate. Dad went mad,'

I looked back at Toby and tears appeared in his eyes. I looked away quickly to try and control my own. The sounds of the restaurant seemed to get louder as our table stayed silent. You could hear the clatter of dishes and cutlery in the kitchen and the noise of people's voices in the dining area. I looked back as Aunt Jean grabbed Toby's hand. He didn't pull away like he usually did. He must miss Mum hugging him, I thought, because now there is no Mum, there are no hugs and kisses. Aunt Jean had tried to when we first came here to live, but Toby had pushed her away, saying she wasn't his mother. I think it hurt Aunt Jean and she rarely tried to hug him now.

'You know the other thing, Aunt Jean?' Toby said.

'What darling?' Aunt Jean asked.

'It was the catch on the gate that was broken. I had shut it, I knew I had.' Toby looked sad and far away. 'If he'd done the work he should've done instead of being drunk all the time, it wouldn't have happened. He always blamed me for things that were his fault, always.' He was back to Angry Toby, his fists clenched.

'I just feel there's so much I don't know about your lives,' Aunt Jean said. 'I hope, for your sakes, that the horrible things you've experienced will fade. I'll try to do my best to give you a better life and be as patient as I can. Hopefully we can all learn to love each other better.' Aunt Jean was crying. I couldn't pass her my serviette; it was all shredded.

It's funny, I thought, how we hadn't talked about any of this with Aunt Jean at home, and here we were in a public place telling secrets. I felt drained and hoped one day we wouldn't talk about the past.

Someone had to take control here, and it had to be me because Toby was crying as well. Oh god, I had to fight the tears. It was a bit like a yawn, see someone do it and the next thing you're yawning as well. Was crying infectious?

'What time is it?' I asked.

'Oh dear, Julie. There's so much I don't know, you poor things.'

We're not things, I thought angrily. 'Don't worry about it, Aunt Jean, don't worry about it,' was all I said.

94

Aunt Jean smiled and patted my hand, not having a clue that she'd said anything insulting. 'I think we ought to have a talk about all this, tonight.'

I knew she meant it, but that didn't mean it would happen, but I said 'sure', anyway.

Aunt Jean must have thought I didn't sound convinced.

'I mean it, Julie, Toby, I'd like to have a talk tonight.'

Toby and I looked at each other; what had he started?

'Whatever,' he said, looking away.

'Uh huh,' I said.

'I'll have to be getting back, I don't really want to leave you, but unfortunately I can't get out of work this afternoon. Will you be all right? Do you want to get a lift home with me after the movie or catch the bus?' Aunt Jean seemed a bit flustered as she stood up.

'We'll meet you,' I said.

'Have you decided on the movie?'

'Yep. The surf one.'

Toby screwed up his face. 'You agreed Toby, next time it's your choice, remember?'

'I'm sure I don't have to say anything about being sensible,' Aunt Jean said.

'Don't worry, we'll be sensible,' I said, trying to hide my exasperation.

'I'll meet you at five, at my office,' Aunt Jean looked at her watch. 'Gotta fly, see you, enjoy the movie.'

'On your broom,' Toby mumbled, but Aunt Jean didn't hear him. I poked him.

We watched Aunt Jean bustle up to the waiter who served us, and give him one of her plastic cards. She waved as she left. Toby and I got up from the table, leaving our mess for someone else. I felt a bit guilty about the shredded serviette.

'Gee, I wish I had one of them,' said Toby.

'What?'

'Those plastic cards, you could buy anything.'

'You still have to have the money in the bank.'

'I know that, I'm not stupid, you know,' he glared at me.

'No, I know you're not.' I hoped this would pacify him. I didn't feel like being stuck with him if he was going to be in one of those moods. I didn't want to argue with him.

We walked out into the street. It was still busy.

'How come you told Aunt Jean about being hog-tied that time?' I asked him.

'Felt like it,' he said shrugging his shoulders. 'Did you see her face? She sure got a shock.'

'I don't suppose her father ever hog-tied her or Mum for punishment.'

'I once asked one of my friends if he'd ever been hog-tied and he didn't even know what it was,' Toby said thoughtfully.

'Ruby would have known.'

'Was she hog-tied too?'

'No, no. A clip across the ear is all she gets sometimes. Ruby showed me a photo of this man who was hog-tied.'

'A photo?'

'Yeah. It was a photo of this old Aboriginal guy who'd been hog-tied by the police and beaten to death. It was over in the West somewhere.' I remembered the photo and the thick file Ruby had shown me. It was a file her mum kept on deaths in custody of Aboriginal people. You wouldn't believe some of the horrible stories. Some were only sixteen years old, just a year older than I was, and they hadn't really done anything wrong, certainly nothing worth dying for. I was almost crying as I told Toby this.

'They beat him when he was hog-tied?' Toby couldn't believe it.

Toby's voice stopped my tears from starting. 'Yep, they said he was uncontrollable. He was this old guy and they said six cops couldn't handle him, so they hog-tied him to get him under control. He died but they reckon he suicided while he was hog-tied.'

'Suicided, how could he suicide?'

I could tell Toby was thinking back to when he was tied like that.

'It would be impossible,' he said. 'Impossible.'

'The cops got away with it, they weren't charged or anything.'

'You're joking.'

'No. They even had video and photos of them beating him when he was tied up, getting him under control, they said.' I paused, remembering another photograph. 'There was this other one, a sixteen-year-old dead boy, and there were fifty-three witnesses who said they saw the police beat him, and those cops got off as well.'

Toby looked amazed. 'Do you think Dad will get off?'

'No. He murdered them. He admitted it to Sergeant Cooper, remember?'

'He better not get off. I'll kill him if they let him out.'

'Toby!'

'I would.' He kicked an empty can along the street. 'How come Ruby has that sort of stuff?'

'Her father died in jail. They said it was suicide but Ruby didn't believe it. Neither did her mum.

They kept a file of all the other deaths in custody because one day they reckoned the truth would come out. Sometimes her mum used to go to meetings about it. Ruby went once. She said it was so sad she couldn't go again.'

'God, I didn't know that.'

'Ruby doesn't like talking about it. She showed me at her house after she told me about her father. You wouldn't believe some of the stuff.' I shivered remembering the boy called John Pat. 'Let's stop talking about it. It's too depressing.'

'Unbelievable,' Toby said. 'Unbelievable, maybe Dad won't get off because he's not a cop and he didn't kill a black person.'

'I don't know if it works like that, I don't know.'

We reached the cinema complex. It was enormous and a whole world in itself. There were queues so I waited in the ticket line while Toby waited in the line for drinks and popcorn. The cinema was full and there were lots of noisy kids throwing things and hooting at anything that came on the screen. There were about four ushers and they kept shining torches on people, yelling at them to get their feet off the seats, stop throwing things and be quiet. A few people were thrown out before the movie began. For the next two hours I was absorbed in the film, the waves and the surfing skills were awesome.

It felt weird when I came out in to the light, from the dark of the cinema.

I expected it to be night, and it wasn't. The movie was excellent. Some of the waves were nearly fifteen metres. The film was made in Hawaii at a place called Outside Log Cabins, where surfing experts say are the biggest waves in the world. Surfers have to be towed out at least three kilometres to the reef. It's the ultimate in surfing to catch a wave there, and I'm going to do it one day. In fact, I might become the first girl to do it because so far only one guy has done it. The only downer about the movie was there was a bit too much kissing, even for me. Toby had groaned every time, poking me saying, Yuck, Boring, and stuff. He wasn't the only one, there was a lot of calling out and boos or cheers would happen whenever the two main stars started kissing. Some people even threw things at the screen.

'Did you like it?' I asked Toby as we walked along George Street.

'Too much kissing.'

'What about the waves?'

'Awesome, totally awesome.' He imitated a surfer on a wave.

'Do you reckon that bit about the tuna sandwich was true?'

'What bit?'

'You know that nerdy guy said sharks can smell one part of tuna juice to two-and-a-half million parts of seawater.'

'How much is two-and-a-half million parts of seawater?'

'I don't know,' I said exasperated. 'The point was that sharks can really smell, so don't eat tuna sandwiches before you go swimming.'

'I don't like tuna sandwiches, but do you reckon it's true?'

'I'm going to look it up in a shark book,' I said.

'What about that guy who was training by running under water with those big rocks?' Toby laughed.

'That sucks, what an idiot, you wouldn't catch me doing that in a million years!'

We walked along the busy street, avoiding as many elbows as possible. There was an hour to go before we had to meet Aunt Jean. I was sick of avoiding people rush by. When they bumped me, hardly anyone said sorry. Rush, rush, rush. What's the emergency? I think Toby and I were the slowest walkers, and I think we got in a lot of people's way. I grabbed his arm and pulled him into the gutter where there weren't as many people. Horns were beeping and abuse came flying out car windows, particularly from taxi drivers. It was hard to think straight.

I wanted everything to just stop for five minutes, so I could get a breath. I felt like it was all too much for me and I started to panic that I was going to stop breathing, and my head was going to explode. I sat down on the kerb. Someone gave Toby a dollar because they thought we were begging. We'd passed heaps of people begging, in front of shops and outside the entrances to the railway stations, and I wondered if that's how I looked, sort of desperate.

'Why did you take his money?'

'A dollar is a dollar,' Toby replied flipping it in the air. 'There's too many people,' Toby said as he got out of the way of this man on a mobile phone, who wasn't even looking where he was going. 'So many idiots.'

'Do you know what you want to do?' I kind of shouted at him.

'Let's find somewhere that's not a gutter to sit and think.'

I got up and went into the crowd again, this time walking faster like I was in the Olympics or something. I don't think I was breathing but I didn't feel so spun out.

We reached a small grey square, with a struggling, caged tree growing out of concrete. There was a little sign at the base of the tree that said it was planted for peace in 1995.

'Doesn't look like peace is doing too well,' I said.

'What?'

'That tree's called peace.' I pointed to the spindly thing.

'Sheesh, we're in trouble.' Toby shook his head.

There was a seat and a little old woman was sitting at one end. Toby and I sat down. The old woman looked scared of us and pulled her bags closer. I smiled at her trying to show we were harmless, just the children of a murderer. The woman gave me a scared look, as if she read my thoughts. She got up and hurried away, looking back once before she crossed the road and disappeared into the crowd.

'Poor thing,' I said.

'Who?'

'That old woman who was sitting there.'

'Why, what's wrong, she got a disease or something?'

'No, she was scared of us because we're teenagers.'

'How do you know?' Toby scoffed not believing me.

'The look she gave us, didn't you see it? She was scared, like she thought we were going to rob her or something.'

'Don't be stupid.'

'It's true, I saw the way she looked. Real scared.'

'Bloody stupid,' he muttered.

A car ran into the back of another car right in front of us. The guy who'd been run into went so red I thought he was going to have a heart attack. The woman who'd run into him was crying. People started beeping at them and yelling for them to get out of the way. Two cops on bicycles came to help sort it out.

'I just think it's sad, that's all.'

'What?' Toby said, 'the prang?'

'No, you idiot. The woman being scared of young people, it's sad.'

'Whatever,' he said, as if he didn't really care what the old woman thought.

We sat for awhile, but it wasn't very satisfactory because it was too smelly and noisy. We wandered into this enormous arcade with heaps of shops that went on forever. I didn't buy one thing because there was too much to choose from, and I couldn't make up my mind on any thing I wanted. I knew I really wanted to buy a surfboard, and I hadn't enough money for one yet, and none of the shops we went into had any. I have to save up for ages to even be able to afford a second-hand one.

'We aren't very good at this, are we?' Toby said.

'What?'

'Knowing what to buy when there's so much choice,' he replied.

'We haven't really ever seen all of the stuff before,' I said, thinking back to the sad shops I'd known in the country, with so little in them. I looked at the moving crowd, blending with the colours in the shops. Patterns of people, I thought as I looked at the variety of faces. Toby was looking at CDs outside a shop. 'Let's get out of here.'

'Let's go and have a milkshake or something. It's nearly time to meet Aunt Jean,' Toby said in a kind of daze.

I saw a man's reflection in the window. I'd seen him looking at us before. I grabbed Toby's arm. 'See that man over there?' I pointed at the reflection.

Toby looked. 'Where?'

I turned around. 'He's gone, but I'm sure he's been staring at us.'

Toby stared at me as if I was crazy. 'There's a million bloody people in the street staring at each other.'

'No, this was different.' I searched hard for the face but it had disappeared. 'Maybe it was nothing.' Toby didn't know why I was so suspicious, but I thought it could be a journalist, or someone who knew who we were. I scanned the crowd once more, but the face was definitely gone. There'd been something familiar and I saw his face again in my mind. Who was he?

CHAPTER 8

Monday Night

We arrived home in time for a swim. I wanted to catch some waves; I had to practise hard if I was going to be world champion. I wished I had a surfboard. The film had inspired me. I was going to find out how much they cost at the surf shop and I was definitely going to classes that taught you to surf properly. I might even join the lifesavers, I thought as I raced down the steps to the beach. They patrolled the beach every day wearing funny little caps. I saw them scanning the sea with binoculars, moving the flags away from the rips, swimming in and out of the break. It looked like a good job, but would I look stupid in one of those hats?

The waves weren't that good, they looked like miniatures, after the giants we'd seen on the screen. There were a few surfers at the southern end of the beach, hanging outside the break, ignoring the swells that came. Body-surfing was impossible because only wavelets rose and fell away. I practised my freestyle up and down between the flags, four strokes and then a breath out the left side of my mouth for twenty, then the right side for twenty. I swam with rhythm and was enjoying the feeling. I stopped and looked where I was. I'd gone way beyond the flags. For a moment I was scared. I tried to judge if I was in a rip. The beach looked so far away and the people had become very small. Don't panic, I told myself, panicking even more. I realised I was drifting quite quickly further and further out to sea. I tried to swim back. What had Aunt Jean told me to do if I was ever caught in a rip? I can't bloody remember. My position was changing, I was sort of heading a bit south. I hope I don't end up in New Zealand, I thought. I panicked again and started swimming frantically towards the shore. What did Aunt Jean say? Why didn't I listen properly? What did she say about rips? I started to cry, I felt hopeless and I thought of poor Toby not having anyone at all. I was getting nowhere swimming. The beach seemed further away and I thought I was going backwards. Then it came to me out of nowhere. Aunt Jean's voice saying tread water and float. Don't swim against the current, swim parallel with the shore until you escape the rip and then swim into shore. Raise one arm in the air and a lifesaver will probably notice.

I started swimming and suddenly a rubber dinghy with an outboard appeared out of nowhere with a lifesaver in control.

'Are you okay?' she asked, as she circled around me.

'Yeah, I'm okay,' I coughed a bit.

'Are you strong enough to get up here?' She reached out and grabbed my arm.

I clambered on, feeling embarrassed. We roared over the waves back to the beach. She came to a stop just before the sand.

'I was between the flags,' I said, 'I just seemed to suddenly end up out there.' I looked at the endless sea and wondered how far out I'd been.

'Don't worry, the rip was sudden before we had a chance to move the flags. You were the fifteenth in the last half-an-hour.'

I suddenly worried about Toby. 'My brother, my brother. Where's my brother?'

'He's up next to the flag with Bill, he was the one who alerted us you were missing.' She pointed to the middle set of flags. 'So far we seem to have got everyone, but I better make sure.' She zoomed off, the stranger who saved my life.

I raced up the sand to Toby. 'God, that was spooky,' I said, collapsing on the sand.

'You just disappeared, one minute you were there and the next I couldn't see you. I kept thinking other people were you and by the time I swam up to them they weren't, then I thought you might have been teasing me,' Toby burst out in a rush of words.

'Thanks for saving me.'

'What happened?'

'You know those rips Aunt Jean is always going on about and how dangerous the sea can be, well I just found out what she meant.' I stared out at the horizon wondering how long I could have lasted just floating. 'I was just swimming up and down between the flags and the next thing I knew I was on my way to New Zealand.'

Toby laughed. 'What was it like being rescued?'

'Embarrassing,' I went red thinking about it, 'but she was cool. She said she's rescued fifteen in the last few minutes and the flags were positioned wrong.'

'Were you scared of sharks?'

'God, Toby I didn't think about that. I probably would have drowned if I'd thought about sharks.'

'I'm never going to go in the water above here,' he pointed to just above his chest.

'Funny, I'd been thinking about joining the lifesavers just before.'

'Are you going to?'

'I might.'

'Are you going to tell Aunt Jean about being saved?'

I thought about it. 'Probably not, it's all over now, why worry her. What do you think?'

Toby looked thoughtfully out to sea. 'Nah, don't tell her, she'll only go on about it and there'll be a boring lecture.'

'Let's get out of here.'

Toby nodded and we gathered up our things.

We went straight home and Aunt Jean suggested that after our showers, we eat tea on the roof. I showered first trying not to remember my fear as the water washed over me. I thought of these 'what if I'd drowned' scenarios but couldn't bear thinking about what Toby would do without me. I dried myself and told myself to not accidentally tell Aunt Jean, because in a way it had been sort of exciting, and I could easily blurt it out.

I went up to the roof, where Aunt Jean had arranged salad things and cold meat. It was still warm but the sun was sinking. I looked over the edge to the sea and there were waves pounding the rocks on the cliffs below. I loved how from the roof you could see the ocean spreading out into the distance, and all these tiled rooftops spreading the other way. I went to the other end of the roof and looked at the fading beach. There were still people jogging up and down and some still in the water. I couldn't see any flags or lifesavers but maybe it was too dim. It was that light that comes before dark where the street lights and promenade lights create a haze, almost like a fog, where everything looks a bit swirly. I went back and sat down at the table.

'I want to talk to you about what you told me today, Toby,' Aunt Jean said with a serious tone in her voice.

Toby looked alarmed. I knew he didn't want to talk about it and neither did I. How come Aunt Jean remembered? Why, hadn't she forgotten like usual?

'Toby?'

'What?'

'Do you want to talk about it?'

'*No*,' he said sharply.

Everything went quiet. I thought I'd better say something. Aunt Jean was buttering bread rolls. I couldn't see her face.

'Sometimes,' I hesitated, trying to find the right words, 'um sometimes, you just don't feel like talking about it. You just don't want to remember,' I said.

Toby came over and sat down.

'Is that how you feel, Toby?' Aunt Jean asked him gently.

'I'm tired,' Toby answered, pulling a bread roll apart.

'All right. I won't make you talk if you don't want to.' She looked out at the horizon. It was quiet, apart from the usual street noises. We all sat, staring.

'I spoke to your lawyer today,' Aunt Jean said breaking the silence. 'I think, Toby, that you better tell her what you told me.'

'Why?'

'It might be important for the court to know these things.'

'Why?' Toby asked, even more puzzled.

'Think about it,' I said, chewing my roll.

He looked at me with wide eyes.

'Does that mean we definitely have to be witnesses?' I asked Aunt Jean.

'It's looking that way I'm afraid.' Aunt Jean ate some salad.

'What did the lawyer say?'

Aunt Jean finished her mouthful before she replied. 'Josephine thinks you may be able to give video evidence.'

'That's good.' I couldn't sit in a courtroom looking at Dad, especially if he was crying. I'd probably cry, or abuse him or something. God knows what Toby would do.

'When will we know what's going on?' Toby asked. 'I mean when is the trial and all that?'

'I think we'll know definite dates tomorrow, that's when the listings for the winter sittings of the court come out.'

I ate, not even tasting what I put in my mouth.

112

Silence descended and I sneaked a look at Aunt Jean. Her face seemed very serious and I knew she was upset that neither of us wanted to confide in her. I mean I did, and I didn't, it was all too soon somehow. I wanted to be able to talk without crying and I wasn't sure if that'd ever happen. I didn't want to think about court, it was all a nightmare that wouldn't go away. I needed to think about something good. I concentrated on the lettuce and tomato on my fork.

'You should have seen the waves in the movie,' I said, remembering the movie had made me feel good. 'They were fantastic, weren't they Toby?'

'Awesome.'

'Some of them were more than fifteen metres. It was in Hawaii somewhere,' I said.

'Fifteen metres sounds terrifying,' Aunt Jean replied.

'Yep, they were immense.' I was satisfied that everything would be all right if we didn't talk about things I didn't want to talk about. 'There was this guy, and everyone said he couldn't do it, but he did. He was towed out by a boat to the break and then he caught the biggest wave in history.'

'Sounds thrilling. I had a bit of a go at surfing when I was younger, but it wasn't for me.'

I looked at Aunt Jean to make sure she wasn't

making fun of me. She looked sincere. Lights started going on around the cliffs.

'I'm going to learn. Is it all right if I meet Jasmine and Phoebe tomorrow?'

'Where?'

'I'm not sure yet. Jasmine said she'd ring tonight.'

'Yes. What'll you do, Toby?'

'There's nothing to do.'

'There's plenty to do, why don't you ring up one of your friends.'

Toby's face lightened. 'Yeah I'll ring Mark,' and he started to race off.

'No you don't. Help clear up and take some of plates down with you,' Aunt Jean called. Toby stopped mid-stride and came back grumpily and gathered up plates and cutlery. 'Now don't run, Toby, just walk.'

I picked up salad bowls and the butter dish, and slowly walked down the stairs to our door. As I opened the door, it felt warmer than the roof. I heard Toby on the phone to his friend. Aunt Jean came in with the stuff from our tea and I started running water to wash up.

'You know about alcohol Aunt Jean?' I turned the taps off and grabbed a glass to wash.

'Oh, we were going to talk about it the other night. Sorry, I forgot.'

'Me too, I just thought about it then.' I rinsed the glass and put it carefully in the dish rack. 'I was wondering if it is like if you have one drink, that then you become an alcoholic.' I paused. 'I mean, at my old school they told us that it's better to say no to drugs, and you know, um, alcohol is a drug.' I stopped and hoped I'd made sense.

Aunt Jean raised her eyes to the ceiling. 'Didn't they teach you about moderation?'

'At my new school, they sort of do.' I didn't want to say I didn't really understand what they meant, because it was new to me. I'd always thought you just said no, and that's what I'd do, mostly because of Dad. I'd tasted beer once when I was about ten, and I didn't like its sour taste and smell. Mum sometimes had a glass of wine, and I'd tasted that and didn't like it either. Before Aunt Jean offered me the glass of champagne, I'd never been in a situation where I had to say no. No one had offered me alcohol at the party, just drugs and I'd said no. Not that I knew that's what the jerk was offering, but even if I did I would have still said no. When Aunt Jean offered me alcohol, I thought I had to be polite and say yes, and that if she was offering maybe it wasn't bad.

'The answer to, If you have one drink will that make you an alcoholic?' Aunt Jean looked at me. 'Of course not.'

'So you don't think I'll be an alcoholic?'

'No, not unless you choose to be.'

'What do you mean?'

'Well Julie, I know there is a real problem with teenage drinking and drug taking . . .'

'I don't drink or take drugs.'

'I'm not saying you do, but you are at an age where you are going to come across them more and more.'

I thought about the party, the drunk kids and the ones taking drugs.

'I think there is a lot of pressure on young people today to get out-of-it.' Aunt Jean looked at me. 'You'll probably be pressured and you'll be told you'll feel great, that it's cool to do it, all those things.'

'I'll say no.'

'Julie, sometimes you mightn't want to say no, you may even feel like experimenting.'

I thought of Phoebe and Jasmine saying they'd tried some drugs.

'What are you saying?'

'Julie, I don't want you to take drugs or get drunk, but I can't stop you. All I can say is that you have to be careful if you do decide at some time to say yes.'

'I won't!'

'I hope you won't, but the point I'm trying to make is that, in moderation, some things are relatively harmless, it's when you start to think it's the only way you can have fun, that's when it becomes dangerous.'

'I don't like out-of-it people,' I said thinking of my father.

'I think a lot of teenagers get hooked up to drinking and drugs because they don't like themselves.'

'And they're bored.'

'There are many reasons. But Julie, I want you to talk to me about these things. I don't want them to become problems for you.'

'They're not.'

'It's still all pretty new and I think temptations will occur. It's Sin City after all.'

I laughed. 'Sin City?'

'That's what they call it.'

'Aunt Jean, did you take drugs?'

I didn't think she was going to answer me, but she finally said, 'I've tried different ones, you know, when I was in my twenties, they were part of our life as well. Every party you went to would smell like marijuana and there always would be drunks.' Aunt Jean put the kettle on. 'Your mother and I both smoked dope for a couple of years, and occasionally got drunk.'

'Mum?'

'Yes, your mother.' Aunt Jean looked out the window and I heard her mumble, 'I hope you don't mind, Joan.'

'I don't believe it, I mean she was always just like a mother.'

Aunt Jean laughed. 'Your mother was more than a mother, Julie, she had a whole life of her own before you came along.'

I stopped and thought about Mum and tried to imagine her smoking. I'd never seen her smoke anything in my life and couldn't believe it. I wondered if she would have ever said anything. Aunt Jean put a cup of tea in front of me. 'Do you think she would have ever told me?'

'Probably, when the time came. The teenage drug problem is not just a city problem but maybe it's something you face sooner here. I'm sure she would have talked to you honestly, when the time came.'

'It's so hard, sometimes I feel so robbed. You know I should be having this conversation with Mum.' Tears came to my eyes.

Aunt Jean stayed silent, and I hoped I hadn't offended her by what I'd said.

'I know you're hurt and you miss your mother,' Aunt Jean paused and took a sip of tea. 'I miss my sister and can't imagine your pain as her daughter, but Julie, I'd like to think you could talk to me about all the issues, sex and drugs and rock 'n roll.'

I blushed and took a sip of tea to hide my red face. Aunt Jean was getting embarrassing again. 'Yeah,' I said to keep her quiet. The tears had stopped half-way down my face.

'You might think I'm an old fogey who couldn't possibly understand, but Julie I work with parents of drug-addicted children, I work with alcoholic and drug-addicted young people and it's so tragic for everyone involved.'

'Don't worry.' Shut up! My head screamed.

'You're so vulnerable Julie, because you are a good girl and you might trust the wrong kind of people. There's bad people out there who like to prey on young girls.'

'Aunt Jean, I don't want to talk about this any more. I got the message.' I sipped my tea.

'I just want to say this, alcoholism and drug addiction are illnesses just like any disease, and addicts need treatment just like any other sick person.'

I wished I'd never started the subject. I didn't want to be an addict and I didn't want drugs. Why did she have to go on about it, as if the next time I went out the door I was going to a drug den or something? What did she mean disease, and could you catch it if you hung around people like that?

'Aunt Jean, if it's a disease, does that mean an alcoholic can't help what they do? You know like they're sick and not responsible?'

Aunt Jean looked puzzled. She opened her mouth to say something and then stopped.

'Well, does it?' I demanded.

'It's a good question, Julie. I'm afraid I don't know the answer. I suppose I believe people have to take responsibility for what they do, but when they become addicted, I'm not sure how responsible they are any more.'

'What about Dad?' I cried. 'He was an alcoholic. Was he responsible?' I burst into tears. I put my hand up for Aunt Jean not to come close. I wanted to get a grip on myself. 'Will I be an alcoholic?' I whispered, finally.

'Oh Julie, Julie.' Aunt Jean started crying. We should call this the house of tears, I thought. Aunt Jean's tears stopped mine. I watched her try to gain control. She took a deep breath that I heard, as if it was my own.

My head was full of questions and I remembered this teacher at school saying, It's not the answers, it's the questions. I didn't get what she meant because surely questions have to have answers. 'It's just that I've got millions of questions and I don't know if there are answers,' I said, thinking of the teacher's round face. 'I just don't want to be an alcoholic. Someone told me it's genetic.'

'All I can say, Julie, is that the small glass of champagne you had won't turn you into an alcoholic. Drinking in moderation is fine. I'm not sure about the genetic bit, science seems to be making genes responsible for every anti-social crime or behavioural disorder. It's so complicated.' She paused. 'My parents, your grandparents, only drank occasionally. Your mother didn't drink often, except for a bit of bingeing in her late teens and early twenties, when she was at uni.' Aunt Jean smiled. 'One day I'll have to tell you a bit about those times. Your father didn't drink much when your mother met him. He spent most of his time working very hard on the farm. I only met his father once, and that was at their wedding, and he did have a very red nose, I must admit.'

'Red nose?'

'It's often a sign of heavy drinking especially in older people.'

I'd be looking very carefully at the colour of people's noses from now on. What made Dad drink? I don't remember him working much. A picture flashed in my mind of a younger Dad, battered hat, sweat staining the armpits of his shirt, the smell of lanolin coming from his nearness, as he walked up the verandah steps. He had two new-born lambs that needed special mothering. I remembered thinking as I looked up at him, that my father was a kind giant. Mum took the lambs from him and called me inside to help with the feeding. I held them, wrapped in sheepskins, while Mum raced around getting the bottles and teats. The pain of thinking about back then was like a dart; it shot through me and made me want to disintegrate.

'Julie, Julie . . .' Aunt Jean shook me. 'Are you all right? You've gone so pale. Stay there. Put your head between your knees. I'll get the Rescue Remedy.'

I felt sick but I couldn't think of anything. My head was pounding and the light became painful. Why didn't I just drown when I had the chance? I felt myself fighting the sea and struggling against it battering me. My hair stood on end and I just wanted dark silence.

'Here, under your tongue.' Aunt Jean dropped the tiny beads of remedy in my opened mouth. Thought stopped and I burst into almighty tears.

'Why, Aunt Jean, why did he do it?' I sobbed.

I saw Aunt Jean take a dose of Rescue Remedy. 'I don't know Julie, I don't know.'

I put my head in my hands and wondered if Dad knew himself. Has he ever told anyone why? I was back to thinking questions, questions, and maybe they might not ever have answers. I wondered about the court case. Dad would have to tell everybody why he did it.

'Do you think we'll find out why in court?'

Aunt Jean rubbed her face with both hands and sort of brushed her greying hair back and sighed. 'I hope so, Julie, but there might not be an answer that we understand.'

'What do you mean?'

'Your father may not remember anything about what happened and he may never have to give evidence.' Aunt Jean looked at me and pulled up the chair next to me and held my hands. 'We're going to have to start preparing for court.'

'I don't understand. Why is there a trial? He murdered them, everybody knows that.' I sat down. 'It's stupid, stupid. He's guilty.'

'Everyone in this country is entitled to a trial, it's our system. They're presumed innocent till proven guilty. In France it's the opposite, guilty till proven innocent.'

'I wish Dad was in France!'

'He'd still have a trial, I know it seems hard to understand, but it's a fairer system than no trial. It protects the innocent too.'

'But what about the guilty?'

'Oh Julie, I know.'

'How long will the court case take, a day or what? Will our pictures or names be in the paper?' I nearly swore, but stopped myself because of Aunt Jean. What if the kids at my new school saw my picture in the paper or on the TV news or something? I'd never be able to go out anywhere again. This time I was certain. Give up the surfing idea, give up every idea, vegetate watching daytime television and looking out the window or hanging about on the roof. That's what I'd do with my life. I had to live to keep Toby alive, I'd sort of thought about that before I was rescued. If I died, then he'd probably die too, and then there would be none of us to remember Mum and Jonathon and Jennifer. I'd do school by correspondence, just so I had something to do. The court case would be the last time I'd ever go out. It wouldn't be the first time anyone stayed in the one house for years. I remembered Toby showing me this news item in this book he was looking at called *Chronicles of the Twentieth Century*. It said, 'Mr Lazy Gets Up' and was about this guy who stayed in bed for twenty-nine years and had to get up when his eighty-year-old mother got sick and couldn't look after him.

Aunt Jean's voice interrupted my thoughts. 'Maybe two weeks, maybe a month.'

For a moment I didn't know what she was talking about and thought she was talking to herself. Then it clicked. The court case. Two weeks, a month. On TV they only took an hour, sometimes two.

'What? That's ridiculous, why does it take weeks?'

'Depends on the number of witnesses called.'

'What witnesses? No one else was there to see, what sort of witnesses?'

'The prosecution calls witnesses for their case to prove your father guilty. The defence brings witnesses to say your father is . . .'

'Not innocent!' I shouted.

'Well, not guilty, because he was insane when he committed an insane act.'

You couldn't argue what he did was sane, but he was still guilty. This was a stupid court. 'He's been insane for years, does that mean they'll let him off?'

'No. It probably means that he'll end up in the hospital section of the prison.'

'Forever.'

'Well sometimes, but if they can prove to the court, at any time, that they are sane, then they may be released.'

One thing about Aunt Jean was that she was honest. She'd answer your questions pretty straight. 'Toby is right,' I said sharply. 'We should just take a gun in to court and shoot him ourselves.'

'Julie!'

'Well, why bloody not? He killed our family.'

Aunt Jean breathed out heavily. 'Look, don't worry about the verdict. You have to start preparing for what you are going to say. I'd like you to see Josephine on Wednesday. You alone first, okay?'

'Well, I don't have much choice, do I?' I hated the whole idea but knew there was no way in the world I could get out of it unless I died and I'd already decided I wasn't going to do that, yet.

'It will take quite a long time to prepare, it's very involved. If I could get you both out of this, believe me I would.'

'Do we have to tell the lawyer things like what Toby told you today?'

'Yes.' Aunt Jean looked at me thoughtfully. 'The more the court knows about your father and mother's relationship, and your father's behaviour, the better.'

'Did anything ever happen to you Aunt Jean, that you felt like you just wanted to die from?'

'Don't say that Julie. You've got plenty of things to live for.'

'Toby,' I whispered.

Aunt Jean jumped up, got the Rescue Remedy, gave me another dose, then hugged me tight. 'Oh Julie, I love you, you're a big strong girl, brave and kind,' she said, tears in her voice. 'You're my favourite niece,' and she hugged me tighter.

'I'm your only niece,' I choked through my own tears. I could hear the waves crashing against Ben Buckler as if they were angry. I felt angry with them. Who hands out the lives? You know, who decided I was born the daughter of a murderer? Why did I get this life? That girl, what's her name, the one on TV who's made it as a surf champion and she's only sixteen, why didn't I get her life? I pulled out of Aunt Jean's hug and walked over to the window.

'I love the sea, the way it sort of takes over your thinking, if you know what I mean.' I stared into the darkness and listened to the waves against the rock. I put my head against the window.

'I think I do.' Aunt Jean was silent and then she stood up. 'I think we've had enough talking for one night. Let's talk more and often, Julie, but not now; I need a good night's sleep.' Aunt Jean joined me at the window. 'You're going out with Jasmine and Phoebe tomorrow, aren't you, that'll be fun.'

'Yeah, but it's not the same,' I said sadly. 'They don't know anything about my past, not like Ruby, you know. They don't ask me much, which is good because I don't know what I'd say. I just don't want them to find out.'

'You won't be identified in any of the media, Julie, you don't have to worry about that.'

127

A great load lifted off me, I felt like shouting 'thank god' to the waves. 'So Jasmine and Phoebe won't find out unless I tell them?'

'That's right.'

'Ruby knows everything, but she won't tell anybody.'

Aunt Jean hugged me again. 'It'll be okay, Julie,' Aunt Jean said, softly. I cried gently, into her shoulder, and smelt that familiar smell of warm gentle skin, that reminded me of when I was very young and snuggling into Mum.

CHAPTER 9

Tuesday Morning

I woke up and looked at the clock. It said nine-thirty. It was very quiet. I hadn't heard Aunt Jean go to work. I got up and peeked down the hall. Toby's door was shut, so he must still be in bed. I felt safer. At least someone else was here; I don't understand why all of a sudden I've turned into a bit of a scaredy cat. Gee, I used to be known as fearless. Maybe it's just that I have never spent much time on my own. I'm cursed by loneliness. The few times I'd been in the flat on my own, I let my imagination get a bit carried away, thinking scary thoughts. I imagined burglars behind the doors and under the couch. I was still a bit wary and on the lookout for trouble as I went to the bathroom. A face in the mirror stared at me and I had to get close to make sure it was really me.

The kitchen was silent and sunlight reflected rainbows around the wall, from crystal prisms that hung in the window. The yellow benches looked like sand and the silver coffeepot gleamed. I sighed as I got a bowl out of the cupboard and poured cereal in it. I grabbed the milk out of the fridge and saw a note asking me to get a few things at the shop on my way home. The shopping money was kept in the biscuit tin decorated with kangaroos and koalas. I looked at the tin that held one end of the recipe books up and lifted its lid and saw ten dollars.

I ate breakfast, hungrily. Weird. Why was I hungry when sleep was all I'd done since I last put food in my body? I felt like going up on the roof because, from the kitchen window, it looked like it was a beautiful day. Blue sky and feathers of clouds heading to the horizon. Sun shining off the sand and water, rainbow sprays cascading from the rocks. I wanted to breathe the sea air.

If I went up to the roof, I'd better do some washing. It didn't take long to pile up around here. I was meeting Jasmine and Phoebe at eleven, on the corner of Hastings Parade. I had ages. I lugged the heavy basket up to the roof and got a bit of a shock to see Mrs Joby hanging out her washing. She and her husband lived in number three.

'Beautiful day,' I said, cheerily.

'Beautiful, my dear. You doing the washing, I see. You good girl.'

'Did you have a good New Year?'

'Very good. My husband and I, we danced till two. Can you believe that?'

I couldn't actually. Mrs and Mr Joby were ancient, I mean they must have been in their fifties or something. 'That sounds great. I went to a birthday party on Saturday night.'

'A party. Well.'

'Yeah. It was great.'

'Oh, you young, you should have as much fun as you can, as long as you don't hurt anybody, that's what I say.'

'I agree, but I still have to do the washing.'

Mrs Joby laughed as I went into the little laundry room. Everyone had a key to their own machines. I unlocked ours and started sorting the clothes. Wash the heaviest first so they dry, I could hear my mum say. I put the first load on. Mrs Joby had gone by the time I walked back out. I looked over the edge.

This is my queendom, and you are all my subjects, I thought, as I waved my arms at the people below. No one looked up, thank god. The sea was calm and there were no waves. Sunbathers lay on the beach and quite a few people were in the water, some just standing staring out to sea. The flags had been positioned. Down in the street a few people hung about doing nothing, but most others seemed to be in a hurry.

A smell rose from the herbs, planted in boxes around the rooftop. A beautiful scent that I breathed in. I remembered Mum crushing peppermint leaves and closing her eyes as she sniffed deeply. It was an image that stayed with me as I scanned the streets with unseeing eyes. I looked into the planter box nearest me and noticed the water dripping out. Mrs Joby must have watered them; everyone shared the rooftop garden. I wish I could remember what things were. I picked a leaf, a minty smell hit my nostrils. Lamb, I thought and threw the leaf away.

The first load was finished and I put the second load on. I hung out the first load and a slight breeze blew the clothes. I went downstairs to see if Toby was up yet. He was sitting at the table.

'I thought everyone was gone,' he mumbled, spooning cereal into his mouth.

'I'm doing the washing. Have you got anything that isn't in the basket that needs washing?'

'Nah. Has Mark rung?'

'I don't know, I've been on the roof, doing the washing, der,' I said dumbly.

'Gawd you're always grumpy.'

'And you always ask stupid questions.'

The phone rang. Saved by the bell, otherwise we'd be fighting as usual. Toby answered it. I put the kettle on. Tomorrow I'd have breakfast on the roof, I decided. I hoped I'd remember, I'd write it in my diary. Toby came back.

'We're going to the skateboard jumps, Mark's mum is picking me up in a minute.'

'Don't break any bones, wear your protector stuff.'

'Yeah, yeah, what are you going to do?'

'I don't really know. Just window shopping I guess.'

'Sounds boring.'

'Oh, shut up Toby, and don't start, I'm sick of bloody arguing and you bloody ought to be as well.' I glared at him. 'I don't go on about what you do.'

Toby's bottom lip looked like it was almost touching his chin, I could see he was thinking about if he should give up, or think of something smart to say. 'That's because I do exciting things,' he said at last.

'Like playing cricket. Sure, very exciting, thrilling in fact.'

'Shut the hell up, it's a good game.'

'All right, all right. Here we go again. Fighting. We've got to try and be nice to each other. It's going to be full-on soon, we've got to get it together, and that means the both of us, Toby.'

'What do you mean?'

'We got to get it together for court and all that and what we are going to say to the lawyer tomorrow.'

Toby erupted. 'Tomorrow. What do you mean tomorrow?'

'Aunt Jean told me last night we've got to see the lawyer tomorrow.'

'What? I don't want to see any lawyer, lawyers suck, I'm going to Aslan's place.'

'We both have to see the lawyer. Together and separately,' I said fiercely. 'I don't make the rules.'

'Who makes these stupid rules? Why do I have to do things I don't want to?'

'Toby don't make it hard for Aunt Jean.'

'Why not? She doesn't like me.'

'Don't be ridiculous. You're her favourite nephew.'

That stunned him. I could see him trying to think of something to say. At last he got it. 'I'm her only bloody nephew, you idiot.'

I laughed. 'Anyway, we've got no choice. Shit, I better see to the washing.' I raced out up to the roof. The machine was just coming to a stop. I was glad this was the last load. There is only so much washing you can do before you get sick of it.

When I got back Toby wasn't there. He'd left his bowl in the sink for me to wash-up. I stamped my foot and started running the washing-up water. I cursed boys and dishes, the bloody van blasting its horn somewhere near by, and the annoying noise of someone's car alarm that just went on and on. Gee, I'd woken up in a good mood and now I was getting really angry; I felt like crying. Maybe I could ring

Phoebe and tell her that I can't go out today, say I've got a virus and that I don't want anyone else to catch it. It probably would be better for them, rather than me hanging around without much to say. I finished the cutlery and wiped down the benches and sink. What would I do? Why did I suddenly feel lonely and unwanted? I looked at the clock, there was still twenty minutes to go before I had to meet them.

I picked up the phone and stared at the receiver. Would Phoebe have left yet? What if she's left already? I better just get ready. I raced and had a shower, a real quick one. I put cargoes on and a baggy top and looked in the mirror, I just looked like any other kid, I suppose. I had to get the last load of washing out. I ran up the stairs two at a time on to the roof, glad that my meeting point was only two minutes away. I hung out the last load and some of the first load was dry, so I took that off and folded it and put it in the basket. It was getting hot. The heat was different to back in the bush. Here it sort of stuck to you, where as there, you couldn't breathe, it was so darn hot. Up on the roof you could always feel a sea breeze. I breathed in the air, and raced back downstairs.

I grabbed the note and ten dollars and ran out the front door, down the stairs out on to the street. I walked quickly to the corner and had to wait about ten minutes and was relieved to see them. I'd begun to think maybe they wouldn't turn up, or that I was on the wrong corner. I was glad to see they were dressed mostly like me, but they had more jewellery on, especially Phoebe's ears where she must have had about twenty earrings.

'I've never seen you wear that many earrings before,' I said.

'I wear this many when I go into the city so no-one hassles me. It works.'

'What do you mean no one hassles you?' Jasmine laughed. 'We get chased out of shops before we even get in them with that look!'

I noticed Jasmine only had about eight and a nose ring. I wondered what Aunt Jean would say if I came home with heaps of earrings and a few nose rings? I almost laughed out loud, thinking about it.

'You need a few decorations,' Phoebe said.

'Yeah,' Jasmine agreed, and looked in her bag. 'Here, put these on.'

I looked at the bits of metal they offered, 'I'm not sure how to make them stick.'

Phoebe and Jasmine laughed. 'You screw them like this,' Phoebe grabbed my ear lobe and started decorating my ear.

'Cool,' Jasmine said when Phoebe finished. 'You look great.'

'Will we catch the Junction bus or the Rose Bay one?' Phoebe looked at both of us.

'Rose Bay, so we don't get held up by the Olympic works. That end's chaos, we could be there for hours.'

'You should hear Mum and Dad go on about the Olympics,' Phoebe said. 'I've had it up to here.' She held her neck. 'They never shut-up.'

'Yeah, my Mum goes on about it all the time, especially when she has to go up Bondi Road for something. I say, Look what's going on in Ethiopia, Mum, before you moan about life here.'

We all laughed, and I wondered if Jasmine really said that to her mother. I felt like I was smiling on the inside. 'My Aunt goes to the protests and never shuts up about it either.' It felt like a bond I shared with my new friends. We got on the bus, showed our student cards and made our way to the empty back seat.

'I don't know why they carry on about the Olympics and everything, it'll be all over by the end of the year. It's queer, they want us to play sport and things but they act as if us having the Olympics is the worst thing that ever happened.'

'Don't start going on about it, I can't bear it.' Phoebe covered her ears and rolled her eyes and pretended she was dying as she slipped down the seat making strangled sounds.

'Hey you, up the back there, what's going on? Are you all right? She's not having a fit or something on my bus, is she?' The bus driver shouted out, his eyes staring at us in the rear view mirror, as he kept driving. I worried that he should be keeping his eyes on the road, there was so much traffic and lights and I didn't want him to crash.

'It's all right,' Jasmine said, waving at him.

'Well don't start mucking up on my bus or I'll throw you off.'

'It's not your bus,' Phoebe said quietly, so that only we heard.

'Shut up,' Jasmine said out the side of her mouth, so the driver couldn't see her in the mirror.

I'd chosen the window and stared at the passing scenery. We made our way along Military Road, past the golf course and the big chimney of the sewerage outlet.

'Isn't that amazing?' Phoebe indicated the sewerage chimney.

'It's a beautiful thing,' Jasmine laughed.

'Can you believe in this day and age that they pump Sydney's shit out into the ocean? My father said that if they'd spent the extra bucks they could have been using it to produce energy and clean water by now.'

'It's disgusting,' I said.

138

'The worst thing is that if the wind and current are going the wrong way, it washes all the crap into Bondi, Tamarama, Bronte and Coogee.'

'Shut up,' Jasmine said.

'Great big turds from Double Bay, Leichhardt, Glebe . . .'

We both said shut up to Phoebe at the same time and covered our ears. Jasmine starting singing.

'And you know what else?'

'Stop it, Phoebe.' We both laughed.

'No listen to this.'

'How bad is it?' Jasmine asked.

'Every year, blokes from the sewerage board have to canoe along the sewer.'

'Shut up!' Jasmine got up and sat in another seat.

'They canoe to Double Bay, then along Liverpool Street to Oxford Street to, get this, College Street . . .'

I got up and sat next to Jasmine. I could hear Phoebe saying, '. . . to Newtown, Annandale, Leichhardt, Glebe and Balmain . . .'

'She's never going to stop,' I laughed. 'Is it true?'

'I think so, her father's an engineer, he probably told her.'

'That's definitely one job I don't want, thanks very much,' I said.

Jasmine laughed. 'You're quite funny aren't you, underneath that seriousness.'

'My Aunt Jean says if you don't laugh, you cry.'

'How bizarre.' Jasmine smiled at me as if we were in a conspiracy.

Phoebe had stopped her sewer talk and we went back and sat with her.

More and more people got on the bus and we were getting more and more squashed. After a few more stops, no one could get any further back. This bloke sat on Jasmine.

'Get off,' she yelled at him, 'get off, you big oaf.'

'Get off,' Phoebe said and pushed him.

'Sorry,' he mumbled, 'I was pushed.'

'Pushed like hell, get off my foot,' Jasmine shouted.

The man looked completely embarrassed but, because the bus was so crowded, the other people wouldn't let him stand up properly. Finally he seemed to get his own space and he wouldn't look at any of us.

'Loser,' Phoebe called to him. He ignored us.

The bus stopped near Taylor Square and heaps of people left through the rear door. We had more room, till the next stop when lots of people got on, for distances they could have walked, and with all the traffic they probably would have got there quicker. I watched us catch up to the same cars at the traffic lights that I'd seen next to the bus at the stop at Oxford Street.

'We better start trying to get off,' Jasmine said.

We pushed our way through, and I couldn't help saying 'excuse me'.

We got off at Park Street and looked in shop windows and pointed out the things we liked. We went in to this big department store and tried on all these different clothes. The shop assistants got fed up, because we didn't buy anything. They gave us looks like we had contagious herpes or something. I avoided looking at their narrowed eyes. Phoebe was so funny, Jasmine and I cracked up, as she tried clothes on and spoke in silly voices. When we tired of one shop, we'd just go to another. I felt like, in every shop, we were followed. I asked the others if they felt it. They told me it happens all the time.

'They think we're going for the five finger discount,' Phoebe told me.

'Five finger discount?' I was puzzled.

'You know, shoplift,' Jasmine answered.

I was shocked. I would never shoplift. Mum had sure drummed in to me not to steal anything from anyone, ever.

'Sometimes kids just do it for a dare and stuff,' Phoebe said. 'It's not worth it, because if you get caught, they take you to the cops and everything.'

We finally got sick of the shops because none of us really had money to spend. There was a loud noise as we walked out into the street. There were thousands of people walking down the middle of the road, shouting. I got scared. There were police everywhere.

'What's going on?'

'It's a demonstration,' Jasmine answered.

'I wonder if it's about Bondi?' I asked.

'I doubt it, there's too many people here.'

People were carrying signs and big banners with rainbows on them. They said, Stop Uranium Mining, End Old Growth Logging, Cut Greenhouse Gases, Capitalism Sucks. I'd seen these sorts of people on the TV news. Dad said they were bludging scum, and now I was here among them. The noise was amazing; people were drumming and chanting. One sign said, 'Woodchipping Old Growth Forest is like Killing Whales for Dog Meat.' What did it mean? I thought about it for a minute. Then I got it, it's like the whales are the giants of the seas, and the forests are like the giants of the land, and it's wasteful to kill them for things you can use other resources for. I felt some sense of pride that I understood.

'Maybe we should join them,' Phoebe said. 'We might get on TV.'

'My mum reckons these people are the real heroes,' Jasmine said.

'Why?' I asked. If Dad saw me on TV, he'd hit the roof, I thought.

Jasmine answered. 'Because they're the ones trying to tell the rest of us to think about the planet.'

'I've never been on a demonstration,' I said, feeling brave. 'I don't go with Aunt Jean to the Bondi ones.'

'I don't go with my parents either,' said Phoebe.

'Let's go,' said Jasmine.

We left the street and joined the demonstration. I looked around me and saw so many different kinds of people, men and women in suits, people with rainbow colours and dreadlocked hair, all sorts of people. The Aboriginal flag led the march, and I could see its distinct colours, through the people. Some of the banners were from trade unions and they looked magnificent held up against the sky. There were even bishops, priests and nuns from the churches dressed in their fine robes. As the march turned into George Street, the noise grew louder. Phoebe started chanting and dancing like a Hari Krishna.

Jasmine and I stopped and tried to act as if we weren't with her.

'Well I suppose she's no weirder than some of them,' Jasmine said to me above the noise of the crowd.

143

Phoebe came back to us.

'Where are we going?' I asked.

'Probably Parliament House,' Jasmine said.

At the end of the street there was a huge line of police. They just stood there with their hands in front of them.

'I don't want to get involved with the police,' Jasmine said.

'Let's go get a cold drink, I'm parched,' Phoebe said. 'I've done my bit for the planet, today.'

We went to a cafe. As I sipped my juice, I wondered if I liked being part of a demonstration. There was sort of a power I felt walking in the middle of the road, holding up the traffic, saying One, two, three, four, What am I here for, with everybody else. I'd had real fun, just like Mrs Joby had suggested.

'What time is it?' Jasmine said as she grabbed my arm.

'Nearly four!' I pointed at the clock on the wall.

Jasmine grabbed Phoebe. 'I've got to be home by five.'

Phoebe looked at her. 'We haven't gone on a ferry yet.'

'I've got to get home.'

I was confused. 'What bus will we catch back?' I asked.

'There's one at twenty-past, we should try and get,' Jasmine answered.

'Look, we've been shopping all day and none of us has bought a thing,' Phoebe said.

We left the cafe and stood next to the red traffic lights.

'I should have got a present for my little sister,' Phoebe grabbed my arm, 'I always get her something.'

'How old is she?' I asked.

'Three. Mum calls her, their last mistake,' Phoebe smiled and turned to me, staring. 'She's gorgeous, you'll have to meet her.'

I almost choked. Three. Jennifer my baby sister would have been three.

'Are you all right?' Jasmine asked, concerned. I looked back at her blankly and she looked at me funny. 'Why don't you get her one of those snow domes we saw in that gift shop?' Jasmine said to Phoebe, turning her back on me.

'Yeah, she'd love that.' Phoebe looked at me, then at Jasmine. I felt like I was under a microscope. I didn't want to think about Jennifer, or Jonathon, Mum, or even Jesse. I tried to stop myself from crying. We crossed the road and stopped.

'The shop's this way,' Jasmine said. They talked about the snow domes in the shop, discussing which one would be best. I listened, and felt I was drifting on this cloud above them. How come Phoebe has a sister the same age as my sister would have been, if she hadn't been murdered? Oh god, I couldn't handle this. It wasn't fair. Why was Jen dead? I had to pull myself together. I was floating above them, below them, while they talked about Phoebe's sister, Bronnie. The waves, I thought, the sea, the sunrises and the sunsets. Phoebe put a photo in front of me.

'That's her, she's gorgeous, don't you reckon?'

I stared blind. The photo merged into a texture and I could see the grains of the photograph but not the face of Phoebe's sister. 'Mm,' I nodded, 'we'd better hurry.' I tried to sound normal. I needed fresh air but, as I breathed deeply, it seemed full of poison. Yuck, what is this air? It stank. I felt closed in and grasped at the side of a building.

'Are you all right?' Jasmine asked, concerned.

'Sure, sure,' I answered, 'It's just crowds, I'm not used to them.'

'Why don't you two wait at the bus stop and I'll run to the shop.' Phoebe looked at us. 'I know which one I'm getting so it won't take me long.'

'Yeah, that's a good idea,' Jasmine said.

'No, no. I want to see the domes again,' I said.

'Let's go.'

We ran up streets, and suddenly I was pushing people out of the way. We got to the shop with the snow domes. 'You go in,' I said, and looked in the window, as they raced inside. 'Which one would you like, Jennifer?' I spoke quietly, pressing my face against the glass. 'Where are you?' I focused on a dome with a surfer riding in it. 'Why aren't you here with me, why can't I buy a present for you?'

Jasmine and Phoebe came out of the shop. 'We got it. We better catch the bus.'

I didn't say much on the bus, but it didn't seem to matter. Jasmine and Phoebe talked to each other. I felt like I wasn't even there. When we got closer to the stop Phoebe asked me what I was doing for the next few weeks. I told them about my friend Ruby coming and they said they wanted to meet her. Part of me felt like, that no way would I introduce them to Ruby because she was my friend, not theirs, but they insisted we do things together. I asked them if they wanted to come to my place for a drink and was surprised when they said yes.

As I stepped off the bus, I noticed a man staring at me. He seemed familiar. I tried to figure out if it was somebody from the bush. I stared back at him feeling like I knew him. Who was he? It looked a bit like the man who'd been staring at Toby and me yesterday.

'Who's that bloke?' Jasmine said.

'I don't know,' I answered truthfully.

'Well, he sure is staring at you like he knows you,' Phoebe said.

'I've never seen him before in my life,' I said and looked away, thinking that's not quite true; he was the same one as yesterday. Was he one of Dad's friends, who had come to track us down? It was funny. I felt like I knew him, but couldn't think where from. Who was he?

'So many people, so many weirdos,' Phoebe said.

I wondered when I'd tell them about my past. As we walked up the street, I kept looking back to see if that familiar face was following. 'We're here,' I said.

'What a great spot,' Phoebe said.

Phoebe and Jasmine loved the flat. Jasmine rang her mother to tell her where she was. Toby walked in and I introduced him, he grunted and disappeared into his room.

'This is a cool view,' Phoebe said, looking out the kitchen window.

'It's fabulous how you can see all the different sides of the ocean,' Jasmine agreed.

'Do you want a cup of tea?' I asked.

'Tea?'

'Have you got some juice?'

I stopped midstream and pretended I was just putting the kettle in its right place.

'Tea?' Phoebe asked. 'Herbal tea, do you mean?'

I froze. I could see the stupid clock of Aunt Jean's with the pretend fish.

'Jules,' Jasmine said, 'Jules, are you all right?'

I looked. 'Sorry, what did you say?'

'Water is fine.'

I wished they'd leave, I didn't want them to look at photos or ask questions.

'My aunt will be home soon,' I said, meaning they should go.

'When does your friend arrive?'

'Wednesday.'

'Ring me and we'll arrange something, go out, you know,' Phoebe said, putting her glass down.

'Yeah, ' Jasmine said, 'we should all get together, go over to Manly or something.'

'I'll ring you.'

'What's she like?'

I was flabbergasted, what was Ruby like? 'She's great,' I finally answered.

'Is that the time?' Jasmine put her glass on the sink. 'Let's go.'

Phoebe looked at me. 'You better ring.'

Phoebe and Jasmine headed towards the front door. 'Maybe we could do something Friday or Saturday?' Jasmine said.

'Sounds good,' I answered, unsure if I meant it.

'I'll ring you,' Phoebe said.

I opened the door. 'Yeah, that'll be great.' I waved as they descended the stairs.

I closed the door. I heard Toby in the kitchen. I looked at the photo of my grandmother in the hall, she looked so different to my mother. Her hair was sort of pressed against her head. I studied her face. Do you know what's happened? I asked, staring into her black eyes. I went to the kitchen.

Toby was making a milk shake. 'Clean up your mess,' I said sternly.

'Yeah, yeah. The Skateboard Park's awesome, really awesome.' Toby's eyes twinkled.

I put the kettle on. I didn't know what to say; sometimes I thought Toby didn't think about it at all. 'How did you go?' I asked, not really interested.

'Wicked. I got the hang of the jumps, no problem.'

'Get any bruises?'

'Just one.' He pulled up his trouser leg. 'See.'

It was a beauty. 'Wow. Did it hurt?'

'Didn't even notice it till later, I hope I can go there again.'

'I'm going to get the washing. Maybe you could vacuum the lounge room and hall.'

'What?'

'Come on, Toby, you know you've been slack lately and I've been covering for you.'

'Men don't do vacuuming.'

'Crap, Toby, and you know it. Anyway you are not a man. It's the deal, you know. Equal tasks for all of us who in this house do dwell.'

'Gee, you're stupid, sometimes,' Toby said disgustedly.

'Just do it,' I ordered.

I went up to the roof. All the clothes were dry. I hummed as I folded them in to the basket. When that was finished I went to the edge to have a look. The sea had picked up since this morning and some of the riders were getting good waves. There were heaps of people swimming. I looked down the street. There he was. The same man. I hoped Aunt Jean would be home soon. She'd send him packing. If her temper was anything like my mother's had been, he'd keep running till he ran out of land. I smiled at the thought of Aunt Jean chasing him up the street. It wasn't funny though. It was wrong. Why did two kids whose father had killed the rest of their family have to live in fear? Why couldn't they just get on with life? It was unfair and once again I wondered as I often did, why was I born?

Toby was vacuuming when I went back inside. Good, I thought, at least I don't have to fight about that. I wondered if I should tell him about the man. I supposed so really. I waited till he turned the

151

vacuum cleaner off. I went over the window and stood behind the curtain, looking down in to the street to see if I could catch a glimpse of the stranger.

'What are you doing?' Toby asked.

'Sshh, come here,' I whispered. 'Don't let anyone see you.' I beckoned him. 'Look, see that man sitting on that seat outside the butchers?'

Toby looked. 'Yeah.'

'Well, when I got off the bus, I'm sure he was watching me. I stared at him and I felt like I knew him from somewhere. I'm pretty sure he was staring at us, yesterday, you know, when I told you.' I couldn't tell Toby, he might be a reporter. I hadn't told him about the newspaper article.

'What?'

'Yeah. I'm sure it's him, he seems familiar.'

'You mean from back home?'

'I don't know. I don't know.' I stared hard at the strange, familiar man. 'Hey, why don't we get the binoculars and look at him and see if you know who he is?'

Toby raced off. He came back with the binoculars, and put them to his eyes.

'What do you think?' I asked Toby.

'Don't know. It's hard to tell when I can only see one side of his face.'

'Yeah. I wonder how we could get him to look this way.'

We were silent.as we thought. 'I know,' said Toby, 'I know.'

'How?'

'We could go on the roof, you could throw something at him and duck and I'll look from a different spot. What do you reckon?'

'Sounds good. I hope I can hit him.' We laughed. 'What will I throw?' We looked around.

'A potato,' Toby said.

I laughed. 'Great, I could take up a few in case I miss with the first one.' I grabbed a handful of potatoes and we raced up the stairs to the roof. Fortunately there wasn't anyone else there.

'How far away do you think he is?' I asked, wondering if indeed I could throw as far away as he was seated, on the other side of the road.

'Not far. You can do it.'

I felt confident, but I'd have to duck fast. I aimed at the back of his head. Toby was behind the top of the incinerator. He could see down but it was unlikely the man could see him.

'Ready, aim, fire,' Toby said quietly. I chucked and ducked. 'You got him,' Toby laughed.

'Can you see him?' I could see he couldn't hold the binoculars straight because he was laughing too much. 'Toby, can you see his face?' I said, through gritted teeth.

'No, I missed it. It was so funny; you should have seen him. You got him fair smack on the back of the head. You'll have to try again.'

'Is he still there?'

'Yeah. He's looking around everywhere, even up here, but I don't see his face long enough. You've got to throw another one.' Toby was trying not to laugh.

'Toby, this is serious.' I looked down at the potatoes. Was I really prepared to throw five more?

'Is he looking this way?'

'No. He is sitting back down, but someone has come and sat next to him.'

'I can't do it. What if I hit an innocent person?'

'This other guy might be innocent for all we know, it doesn't matter. Just aim like you did last time,' he laughed, 'at the back of the skull.'

'Well, get ready.' Why was I doing this? What would Aunt Jean say if she knew I was throwing potatoes off her roof at some strange man? 'This is the last one, Toby, so you better get a good look. Ready?' I peeked over the edge. I could see him sitting there. Could I be lucky and hit him twice in the head. I threw.

'You got him,' Toby said with delight. 'Gee, you are a good throw, same spot, exactly same spot.'

'Did you see his face?'

154

'Yeah, but I don't know him. Never seen him before. Hold on, he looks like somebody.'

'That's what I thought, somebody.'

'Yeah, I don't reckon I know him, but he does look like what's his name.'

'Who?'

'You know, that bloke that used to serve petrol back at the garage.'

'Don't be stupid.'

'No, I mean it, you know that bloke Dean.'

'Don't be stupid Toby, that's not Dean.'

'He looks like him.'

'I know what you mean, he's got that familiar look about him. I know him from somewhere, I just don't know where.' I was puzzled. 'Is he still looking this way?'

'No. He's moving off the seat. Duck, he's looking.'

I just got down in time. 'Did he see me?'

'No. He's going.' Toby looked at me, and then he put his eyes to the binoculars. 'The other bloke is talking to him. He's getting up. They're going down the hill, I can't see his face, just his profile.'

'Do you think Aunt Jean will notice some potatoes are missing.'

'No way,' Toby said scornfully. 'Who counts potatoes?'

'He's gone,' I said.

'It was the deadly potatoes.'

'No,' I mused, 'he'll be back, and next time I think we need something heavier.'

'You don't mean?

'Yes, Toby, we'll have to use the secret weapon.'

Toby looked at me. 'What's the secret weapon?'

'Think, what's better than a potato?' I looked at him. 'Well, what's greater than a potato?'

Toby stared at me and I knew he was thinking. 'An AK47 and a bazooka,' he said as if he was the first person to ever think of it.

'Bullshit, Toby. Is that organic, can you just go and find an AK47? No, it has to be something you know that's right there in front of you.'

Toby stared into the sky. 'What's better than an AK47?'

'Do you really want to know, and if I tell you, it's a secret on price of death, do you understand?'

'Price of death?'

'Yes, Toby, the information is top shelf. Only those that can be trusted with such a big secret can know it, if you know what I mean.' I looked at him. 'You're lucky I'm going to tell you.'

'Are you going to tell me?'

'If you promise that once I tell you, you'll swallow it, and keep it to yourself?'

'I promise.'

'On what?'

'On the bones of all my ancestors,' Toby looked earnest.

'Onions,' I said, 'next time we'll use onions.'

Toby looked at me as if I was mad. I gave him the look that said I was serious. He walked up and down. 'Yeah, onions half-peeled, so they make him cry.'

'We better go count them,' I said, 'make sure we've got a supply.'

We walked down the stairs to the flat. As I opened the door, I could tell Aunt Jean was home. 'Don't say anything in front of Aunt Jean,' I warned him.

'No way!' he replied, indignantly.

CHAPTER 10

Tuesday Evening

'Hi,' I said to Aunt Jean, as Toby and I walked into the kitchen.

'Hi, what have you been up to?' Aunt Jean asked.

Toby and I looked at each other guiltily. 'I had a great day with Phoebe and Jasmine.'

'What did you do?' Aunt Jean sounded uninterested.

'Oh, mostly window shopping and stuff. It was fun.' I looked at Aunt Jean. She looked dreadful. Her face was drawn and it looked as if she had aged since this morning. 'Are you all right, Aunt Jean?' I was concerned. 'Would you like a cup of tea?'

'Thanks Julie, that would be lovely,' she sighed.

'What's up? Did you have a hard day?'

'Pretty hard. A cup of tea would be nice, thanks.'

Something was bothering Aunt Jean. I hadn't seen her look this bad since the funeral. I wasn't sure what to do. Should I ask her, again, what's up? I suppose if Aunt Jean wanted to tell me she would. I'd just stay quiet. I concentrated on not making a noise.

'Onions are better than potatoes,' Toby said.

I glared at him, couldn't he see something was up with Aunt Jean? God, I hoped no one had seen me hurling potatoes off the roof. What if this was what was bothering Aunt Jean? Maybe someone had seen us and had told Aunt Jean. Oh god, I hoped it wasn't the potatoes.

'Would you like a biscuit?' I offered. 'I'll put some potatoes on.' I paused to see if there was any reaction to the word, 'potato'. 'We could have them with salad and chicken.'

'Sounds good, Julie. Thanks very much. You know I really appreciate the effort you put in, doing your share of the housework.'

I was embarrassed. 'Yeah, well it isn't hard to make a salad, cook potatoes.'

'No. It's more than that Julie. I'm really proud how well you have adapted to living with me, with all the new things you have to deal with. I know you miss your Mum, and you see me as the only relative you have, but . . .'

I didn't want to talk or think about Mum. Why was Aunt Jean bringing it up now?

Toby looked at me and I shrugged my shoulders. He went to his room.

'You should have seen this demonstration, I saw today,' I said.

Aunt Jean looked a bit surprised. 'I saw it out my office window.'

'Did you see me?'

'Julie!'

'What?'

'Were you there?'

'It was an accident. We were just walking along and then I heard this noise,' I looked at Aunt Jean. 'I've never seen anything like it, except on TV.'

'So you joined in?'

'You demonstrate!' I said accusingly. Aunt Jean looked away.

'Yes, yes, but I didn't know you were going on a demonstration.'

'Phoebe and Jasmine agreed with the protestors, so we joined in for a little while.'

'So you did it because Phoebe and Jasmine did it?'

'Well sort of, I suppose.' I was a bit confused.

'Julie, what do you think yourself?' Aunt Jean spoke quietly.

'About the banners and things?'

'Yes. What the demonstration was about?'

'You mean logging old-growth forests and mining uranium and things.'

'Yes.'

'I think it's wrong.'

'Why?'

'I just do, that's all.' I didn't know what to say.

'If you do agree, then you ought to know why. I don't mean to sound like I'm lecturing, but if you meet someone who doesn't agree with you, it helps if you know what you believe yourself and why.'

'What do you think?'

'Oh, I agree with what the demonstrators are saying. In fact, I marched for the very same things over twenty years ago.' Aunt Jean laughed. 'I'm glad that there is another generation taking over the protests. You get worn out.'

'Aunt Jean, you mean they're still protesting about the same things?' I was shocked.

'Afraid so, Julie.'

I stared out the window. There was a ship on the horizon. Slowly heading south. I thought, is the world crazy, or am I? I turned back to Aunt Jean.

'It's a strange world,' I said.

'It's the only one we have, we've got to make the best of it,' Aunt Jean said. 'I'll shower and then I want to talk to both of you.'

'Why?'

'I'll tell you after my shower.'

I tidied up a bit. My mind was all over the place. I still felt a bit scared that it might be about the

161

potatoes. I went and looked in the potato holder. Could you notice that some were gone?

Aunt Jean came back in. 'Is Toby on the computer, again?'

'I think so. I told him you wanted to talk to us.'

'I'll speak to you alone first.'

Then Aunt Jean started crying. God, it's so hard to know what to do when adults start crying. I mean, I know they cry, but you don't see it happen much. I mean, Mum sometimes cried in front of us, but mostly she cried alone in her room, where I could hear her sobs at night. What should I do?

'Aunt Jean, Aunt Jean, what's the matter?'

Aunt Jean tried to sit up straight. Her face was streaked with tears. I got her a hanky. She wiped her eyes slowly, then scrunched the hanky up to them. I could tell she was still crying, because her body shook.

'Oh dear, I'm so sorry, Julie, I'm so sorry.'

I didn't know what to say. For some reason the man sitting on the seat popped in to my head. I knew it wasn't about the potatoes. Aunt Jean wouldn't be that upset. 'What's the matter, Aunt Jean?' I grabbed the Rescue Remedy and offered it to her.

Aunt Jean stopped crying, but I noticed she scrunched the hanky up in her hand. Toby came in. I sort of gave him a sshh look. He shrugged and walked out again.

'I'll make us another cup of tea.' I sounded as normal as I could. I really was on edge about what could be wrong with Aunt Jean. I sort of tiptoed around, not wanting to disturb her. Naturally I knocked the cup over. The clatter made me jump even though I saw it happen. 'Sorry, clumsy.'

Aunt Jean stared out at the sea. She looked like Mum side on. Her hair was different. Mum's had been long, sort of wavy. Aunt Jean's was short. She'd told me if she grew it it'd be like mine. I turned the potatoes off and strained them in a colander. I wondered if Aunt Jean was going to tell me what was up? I hoped so, I felt useless.

I placed a cup of tea in front of Aunt Jean. I could tell she was a million miles away. I held my breath and took a sip of tea. It was too hot and it burnt my mouth. 'Ouch!' I said involuntarily.

'Pardon?'

'The tea's hot.' I stared out the window. I wondered if the man was still there. That bloody man, he'd really got under my skin. Why couldn't I forget him? Get him out of my mind now, I order you, brain. That is what my counsellor said. I could get rid of unwanted thoughts by telling them to go away. Well I was ordering that bloody man out. I stared. Was he gone?

'Julie?'

'Yes.'

'Well, Julie, it is hard to know where to begin.'

'At the beginning,' I offered.

Aunt Jean smiled. 'Seems logical,' she laughed. 'I think I'll tell you both at the same time.'

'Is it about the lawyer tomorrow? I already told Toby.'

'It is not about tomorrow, but we do have to talk about that as well. Toby.' Aunt Jean called. 'Toby.'

'What?' Toby answered.

'Will you please come here and don't say what, it sounds rude.'

God, that sounded like Mum, I thought. Toby dragged himself into the room.

'Sit down, please.'

'What now? I do try to remember to put the toilet seat down, if that's what you're going to go on about.' Toby was aggressive.

'No, that isn't what I want to talk about.' She looked at him sadly. 'I don't mean to nag you about the seat Toby, I just wish you'd remember, then I wouldn't have to go on about it.'

He had that You're a dried up old prune look. I wondered if Aunt Jean knew what he was thinking, like I did.

'Whatever,' Toby finally said. 'Is it about the lawyer? Julie already told me, and I'm going to Aslan's place.'

'It isn't about the lawyer, but I'm sorry Toby, you can go to Aslan's another day.'

Toby glared at me as if it was my fault. I shrugged my shoulders.

'Have they set a court date?' I asked.

'I read the listings today. June the sixth.'

'What about the other?'

'The other?'

'You know, video evidence and all that?'

'There still hasn't been a ruling, I'm afraid. We should know by the end of the week.' Aunt Jean looked tired and even older. Oh god, I thought. It's living with us kids. We've already made her look older, and it has only been a couple of months. What would she look like in a year. Our grandmother?

'Does anyone want to eat now?' I asked, hoping to change the atmosphere.

'I'll help,' said Toby. At last he got it. Something was up with Aunt Jean. She wasn't her usual self.

'What's up?' Toby whispered to me, as he bent over the cupboard, getting out plates.

'No bloody idea.'

'Freaky.'

'You can say that again.'

'Freaky.'

'Toby don't.' I almost laughed. Not because it was funny, but because I was tense.

We put the food on the table. It looked good.

'Thank you,' Aunt Jean said. 'This looks great.'

We ate mostly in silence, occasionally Toby or I mentioning something about our day.

Aunt Jean seemed a bit more relaxed, but there was still this strained look around her eyes.

'How about when we finish here, we go up to the roof and have our talk?'

'Flying potato roof,' Toby said. I could have slapped him. I had to stop myself from laughing so I didn't spit out a mouthful of food.

'Pardon, Toby?' Aunt Jean looked puzzled

'Oh, nothing. Just sounds good.'

We finished and cleared up. 'Leave the washing-up,' said Aunt Jean, 'it must be my turn.'

'We don't mind,' I said. Toby stared at me as if I was mad. I gave him the anything to delay talking look. He got it.

'No, we don't mind,' said Toby.

Aunt Jean was shocked. 'No, no, I mean it, leave it. I'll do it later.'

We had no choice, Aunt Jean wanted to talk, now. Didn't adults realise that we don't listen much to what they say? We don't like talk, talk. Sometimes I just go deaf.

'Is it all right if I rinse out a few things first, then I can hang them out while we are up there?' I said as a last resort at delaying.

'No, come on, let's just talk. You can do that later.'

Oh dear, this sounded serious. We followed Aunt Jean up to the roof, giving each other what's-going-on looks. As we walked out on to the roof, I thought how much I loved it; it was like I was on top of the world. The air was a bit thinner and you could see forever. We sat down and all looked out to sea, as if drawn to it like a magnet. Clouds gathered in an angry rumble on the horizon.

'We might be in for a storm,' Aunt Jean said. 'Probably not on land but definitely out to sea.'

'Great,' I said. I'd loved watching lightning in the distance, it was spectacular out at sea highlighting the white caps of the waves.

It was silent on the roof, although you could hear street noises and the faint crashing of the surf. I could tell Aunt Jean was trying to start this talk, but she seemed to be having great difficulty. Toby walked over to the edge. He looked back at me alarmed.

'Potato Head is still there.'

I ran over and had a look. Sure enough, Potato Head was back on the seat outside the butcher's.

'What did you say, Toby?' Aunt Jean asked.

Toby and I looked at each other. Did she know about the potatoes? 'We better get this over and done with,' I whispered to Toby.

'Nothing, Aunt Jean,' Toby lied.

'Come back here and sit down the both of you.'

We meekly went back and sat down. I looked at my bare feet. They were much more interesting than looking at Aunt Jean.

'Today I had a phone call,' Aunt Jean began.

'So did I,' Toby butted in. I gave him my sternest shut-up-your-face look. He pulled a face at me. 'That's an improvement,' I said to him.

'You two, please,' Aunt Jean said. Her sharp tone of voice made us both stop. 'This isn't easy for me, I'm finding it hard to believe myself.'

Oh, oh, here she goes. How could we throw potatoes at a stranger? He was probably going to sue us for assault. I could see it now. He knew Aunt Jean was a lawyer. We were really in for it. My imagination was running berserk. Would she send us away to a home?

'As I was saying, today I had a phone call. It was from a man.' Aunt Jean looked out to sea. 'He says he is your father's younger brother.'

'What?' Toby and I said at once. We looked at each other.

A memory came out of nowhere. I was about eleven. Mum used to always go on about putting her photos in albums. They were under my bed in boxes. One day, I helped her. In one box were Dad's photos and I remembered one photograph, clearly. It was of Dad with his arm around a young man. Dad was in his soldier's uniform. I asked Mum who the other person was. Mum told me it was Dad's younger brother, Wayne. I asked her how come we'd never heard of him or ever met him. Mum said Dad says he's dead and that I was never to mention him. I had promised Mum I wouldn't say anything to Dad, or anyone. I remember at the time wondering how he died and how come Dad never talked about him, or even mentioned him.

'Julie?' Aunt Jean asked.

'I thought he was dead,' I said.

'You mean you knew about having an uncle? ' Aunt Jean asked, sounding surprised.

'I don't know anything, no one tells me anything,' Toby said angrily.

'I thought he was dead,' I said again.

'What do you mean?' Aunt Jean asked.

'How come you knew?' Toby asked me accusingly.

'It was a photograph,' I said, seeing it again. 'It was Dad with his brother.' I looked at them both. 'Mum said it was just before he was sent to Vietnam, Dad, I mean.'

'How come you never told me?' Toby demanded.

'Mum said not to tell anyone,' I answered. 'Not even you. I'm sorry Toby.'

'How come you thought he was dead?' Toby asked.

'Mum said it.' I thought back. 'Well she didn't say actually he was dead, she said, Dad says he's dead.'

We all looked at each other.

'Why did Dad say he was dead?' Toby said. 'Maybe he's a murderer like Dad, maybe it runs in the family.'

'Toby don't be ridiculous,' I said.

'That's not it, Toby,' Aunt Jean said, 'He wants to meet you.'

Potato Head sprang in my mind like a jack-in-a-box. 'I've seen him,' I said. Toby looked at me. I mouthed Potato Head to him. He raced over to the edge. 'He's gone.'

'Who has gone?' Aunt Jean asked.

I told her about the man, leaving out the part about the potatoes. I figured she'd just thought we'd nicknamed him for our own warped reasons.

'It's possible,' she said.

Toby came back from the edge. 'I'm sick of this, what sort of family was I born into?' He had tears in his eyes. 'I don't want to meet him.'

No one prepares you for reality, I thought. I just wanted to be someone else. Anyone else, but me, someone who had a normal life. A life where you didn't have to worry about other people knowing the

170

truth about your family. Not feeling ashamed of your mum and dad. I was angry with them both for their lying; their fighting, for being my parents. I wanted to hit something. There was some washing on the line. I got up and went over and punched a sheet.

'Oh, bloody hell,' said Aunt Jean, wringing her hands together. 'I wish this hadn't happened. I told him I'd tell you, but it would be up to you two, from there.'

'I just can't believe for fifteen years of my life, I've had this uncle, I've never met, because I thought he was dead.' I shook my head in disbelief.

Toby walked back to the edge. 'He's back,' he said.

'He wants to meet you.'

Toby and I were silent.

'How come he knows where we live?' Toby asked.

'I told him I lived here, not the actual address, he must have looked it up in the phone book,' Aunt Jean answered.

'I'm going to become a nun,' I said. 'I am.'

'Julie, I don't think you need to be that dramatic,' Aunt Jean said.

'What do boys join if they want to be a nun?' Toby asked.

'Toby,' Aunt Jean looked at him, 'you've nothing to hide from, you haven't done anything to be ashamed of.'

171

'Being born into this family is enough shame for anybody.'

'Toby, Julie, let's have a cup of tea and figure out what you want to do. You have to see Josephine at ten. I wanted to prepare you a bit for the things she might ask you, but . . .'

'I'm too tired, tonight,' I said.

'Me too,' Toby jumped in.

'That makes three of us,' Aunt Jean replied. 'I trust Josephine, you'll be fine.'

'I'm going to stay up here for a while,' Toby said.

I knew he was going to watch the man, who might be our uncle.

'Wayne,' I said to Aunt Jean. 'I don't know if I want to meet him or anything.'

'It's up to you. You'll have to decide for yourselves, I won't make you do anything you don't want, and I certainly won't make you meet Wayne, if that's what you decide.'

'That's not true,' Toby shouted out. I didn't realise he was still listening.

Aunt Jean went over to him.

'We have to talk to the lawyer, we have to go to court. I don't want to do any of that but I don't have a choice,' Toby shouted.

Aunt Jean put her arms around him. I could tell he was resisting, then his body softened. He started

172

crying. Aunt Jean held him while he sobbed. I felt tears coming to my eyes. I resisted them turning in to a flood. Breathing, Julie, breathing, I whispered to myself.

After a while it went quiet. Toby's sobs stopped. I went over to where they were standing.

'Toby,' I said quietly. He looked at me. 'Mr Potato Head,' I said and he burst out laughing.

'What is this about potato head?' Aunt Jean asked.

'Oh nothing. I'm going to make a drink.'

I left Aunt Jean and Toby standing together at the edge of the roof, looking out to sea. I had that everything is unreal feeling. A swirling sea of silence filled my head as I walked down the stairs. I wanted peace, that's all, and a normal life. I didn't want to go to court. I didn't want to think about it again. I wanted it to be all over. I wanted it all to go away but, as I opened the door, I knew it wouldn't.

As I put the kettle on, I told myself to think of something good, something that would make me happy. I thought Ruby's arriving tomorrow, and that made me smile. I could talk to her. Ruby would listen. I could say anything and I knew she didn't judge me.

The phone rang. I answered it.

'Hi, girl, it's me.'

'Ruby!'

'The one and only.'

'I was just thinking about you. You must be psychic.'

'I am,' Ruby laughed.

'I miss you Ruby.'

'Well you won't be missing me long, because I'm on that train tomorrow.' Ruby paused. I could hear her talking to someone else in the background. 'Can't talk long, its Auntie Joy's phone.'

'I'm so glad you're coming, the train gets in it at four doesn't it?'

'Yeah and you better be there. I haven't been to that big city since I was a baby.'

'I'll be there, don't you worry. I'm so glad you're coming.'

'See you then, don't forget, four at Central station. I gotta go, Bucky wants the phone.'

'I won't forget, I can't wait to see you tomorrow.' I hung up feeling much better.

Aunt Jean came in to the kitchen as I finished making the tea.

'Ruby rang. She'll definitely be here at four,' I told her.

'We'll be finished with Josephine by then.'

'We can't be late, Aunt Jean, Ruby would die.'

'Don't worry, we won't be late. I'm glad Ruby is coming, she'll cheer you up.'

'I sometimes feel like I can't cope any more, and now this Uncle Wayne thing. I mean why did Mum want me to think he was dead, why didn't she tell the truth?' I looked at Aunt Jean for an answer. She should know, I mean she's an adult, she knows how their minds work and why they sometimes lie to kids.

'I can't answer, because I don't know. I can only guess.' Aunt Jean sighed. 'Wayne wasn't around by the time your mother met your father. Apparently he became involved with an Aboriginal woman called Aloma and went and lived with her on the reserve.'

'What?'

'It was while your father was in Vietnam.'

'Did Wayne tell you this?'

'We only talked for ten minutes, I was very busy. He told me that this was what caused the falling out with his family.' Aunt Jean looked thoughtful. 'If you do meet him, he'll tell you his story himself.'

'I don't know. Everything is complicated enough.'

'You don't have to make up your mind straight away. Wayne is going back to the country, tomorrow.'

'Where?'

'Back to his old place, your old place.'

'What do you mean?'

'I mean Wayne is going back to rebuild the farm.'

I was stunned. I hadn't really thought about the farm, or the sheep and everything. It was like I felt after the house was burnt, everything was gone but I realised there were thousands of hectares and hundreds of sheep still sitting there. Some of the sheep must be wondering where we were. I hoped they could find food and water. I wondered if any had drowned in the floods after we left. I suddenly felt really bad that I hadn't thought of what the sheep were going through, but if I started caring about the sheep, the other stuff, my family, school, everything I'd lost would cause me such grief that I would become a mess. There wasn't time at the moment to crumble.

'Julie, even though your mother and father owned the farm . . .'

'Mum?'

'Yes, Julie, she owned half the farm. At the moment, I suppose the property is your father's, but there will be no settlement of the estate, till . . .'

'After the trial?'

'Yes. Wayne has your father's authority to go and try and salvage something of the farm.'

'Has he seen Dad?'

'Yes, he visited him, yesterday.'

I was silent. Thoughts crashed against each other. Does he know anything about sheep? Does he drink? Is he like Dad? I didn't know what to think.

'This is all too much, you know, too much.' I banged my head with my fist.

'Julie.' Aunt Jean's eyes wandered to the bottle of Rescue Remedy on the fridge.

I laughed. 'I suppose nothing else could possibly go wrong, I mean everything possible has.'

'I hope Toby comes in soon. You've both got a big day tomorrow.'

'I'm going to have a shower and go to bed.'

I thought of Wayne, and I knew it was Mr Potato Head. That's why I thought his face was familiar. A memory of a glimpsed photograph, years ago. I brushed my teeth.

Would he try to meet me out on the street? Would he just butt into my life? I had to tell Aunt Jean to tell him to not come near me. I didn't want to meet him, yet.

'Goodnight, Aunt Jean.' I went and hugged her. 'I don't want to meet him and tell him to stop following us.'

'I've got his mobile number. I'll give him a ring later. Goodnight, Julie.'

CHAPTER 11

Wednesday Morning

When I awoke, I remembered I'd had some weird dreams, but I couldn't put them together. Just images of a wild ocean with enormous waves and lightning and this bottle, bobbing up and down, and a bell ringing over and over, somewhere. I don't remember if I was in it or what? I'm not sure what dreams are, but I reckon they're important. Aunt Jean and Toby were already up when I walked in to the kitchen. Toby was reading the back of the cereal box for the hundredth time.

'Did you sleep all right?' Aunt Jean asked.

'Sort of, I had some weird dreams, but I can't remember them clearly.'

'Me too,' said Toby. 'I was on this little boat and there was a fierce storm. I had to get to this island but I kept going round and round even though I was rowing straight ahead.' He looked at me puzzled.

'Well, they say water and things means emotions,' said Aunt Jean.

Toby had that look. I knew he thought Aunt Jean

178

was a bit of a kook with some of the things she believed in.

'Do you know about dreams?' I asked.

'No, not really, just a few things I've picked up. Dreams often play an important part in other people's cultures. We get abbreviated meanings in magazines, you know the Stars, all that sort of thing.' Aunt Jean looked like she was getting exasperated. 'Oh god, what am I saying?'

'Nothing. I wish I could remember all of my dreams, not just like flashbacks. I just remember the ocean, lightning, a bottle, and hearing this bell ring, over and over.' I tried to think and recapture more, but nothing came.

'We ought to get a book on the subject from the library,' Aunt Jean said.

'Yeah, I've wanted to for ages, but keep forgetting. Maybe today?'

'I'm not sure how long it will take with Josephine. I've told her about Ruby arriving. If there is time, we'll go to the library.'

'Do you mean it could take all day?' I asked. How could we talk all day about Mum and Dad or even us?

'It could take a couple of hours.'

I wondered if the lawyer would ask us questions, or if she would just wait for us to say something.

She'd wait for hell to freeze over if she waited for me to spill the beans. Mum had taught us well about secrets. I knew now that Mum must have had heaps of secrets she kept from me. I was resentful and for a minute I started feeling terrible, sick and everything. I looked at Aunt Jean for some comfort.

'Will you be there?' I asked.

'I can't, I'm sorry. I may be called as a witness as well.'

'You?' I was shocked.

'Yes. They might want to ask me questions about my sister, your mother.' Aunt Jean looked away. I noticed she'd bitten her lip when she'd said 'sister'.

'Do they have to question everybody Mum knew or something?' Toby asked exasperated.

'No, no.'

'Are we catching the bus?' I asked hoping we weren't.

'No. I'll take the car. Remember we have to pick up Ruby at four. She may have a big suitcase or something. It will be easier in the car.'

'I'm going up on the roof to see if he's still there,' Toby said.

For a moment I didn't know who he was talking about. It then came back, Uncle Wayne. 'I'll have a quick shower,' I said. I didn't want to know. Even though I'd had a shower last night, I felt like I needed one now to calm my nerves and somewhere private to think. I was as nervous as hell.

I looked at myself in the mirror. My eyes looked closer together today. What would I wear? What do you wear when you visit a lawyer? I turned the shower on. I let the water wash my thoughts down the plughole.

I chose a blue skirt and black top. It didn't look right. A black skirt and blue top.

'Is this okay?' I asked Aunt Jean.

'Fine. You look fine.'

There must be something wrong, I thought, if a fossil thinks I look fine.

'You'd better take a coat. It might rain,' Aunt Jean said.

I looked out the window and sure enough the clouds were closer. If it rained here, it could bucket down. I'd been caught once before and had been drenched. Toby came back.

'He's not there,' Toby said, sounding disappointed. He had the same clothes on as usual. It seemed so much easier for him just to throw on anything. He didn't spend hours in front of the mirror. I had that feeling once again that it was so much easier for boys. Everything, I thought. Maybe he would start worrying more as he got older. I hoped so. It shouldn't just be us girls who have to worry all the time.

We got in the car. The traffic wasn't too bad until we got closer to the city. We didn't talk much. The radio was on a classical station.

'You can turn it on to your station if you want,' Aunt Jean said.

Surprisingly, I didn't want to. The music was calming and my stomach was already in enough knots. 'It's fine.'

'Toby?' Aunt Jean said, being fair.

'What?' He obviously hadn't been listening.

'Do you want different music?' I asked him.

'I don't care,' he said and went back to looking out the window.

We parked at Aunt Jean's work. We walked around the corner to the lawyer's office. Aunt Jean came in with us. We'd met Josephine once before and I'd liked her. Aunt Jean arranged to meet us when Josephine was finished. I went first. I suppose it's because I'm the oldest. The legal secretary took Toby with him. I saw him seat Toby at a computer.

My mouth felt like the bottom of a budgie cage, as they say. My stomach was acting if it had entered the trampolining at the Olympics or something. It was doing triple twirls and somersaults. I didn't know if I'd be able to talk. What if I'd lost my voice? I wouldn't be able to say anything. I could feel the perspiration dripping down from under my arms.

'Would you like a drink?' Josephine asked, as she pointed me to a chair.

'Yyy . . . hh . . . yyes.'

'Are you scared, Julie?' Josephine looked at me with the greenest eyes I had ever seen.

'A bit.'

'A bit?'

'A lot.' I laughed. Not a funny laugh but a stupid laugh almost like a guffaw. I had to get myself together. Breathe, I said crossly to myself.

Josephine pressed the buzzer and asked her secretary to bring in some morning tea.

'I have no idea how hard this is for you,' Josephine spoke honestly. 'I can't even imagine what it must feel like to have such tragedy and to lose most of your family. I'm not going to pretend I understand. My job is to try and get justice for you and Toby. To represent your interests as best I can.'

I felt scared. 'It's horrible,' I whispered.

The secretary, whose name I discovered was Richard, brought in a tray.

'Tea, coffee or a soft drink?' he asked.

'Tea, thanks.' I was glad for the interruption.

'Same here thanks, Richard,' Josephine shuffled some papers and brought out a clean pad and wrote a few things on it. 'Have a biscuit if you want.'

I couldn't eat a biscuit in front of them.

'Do you want me to order some lunch?' Richard asked.

'Leave it for now, thanks.'

'Your brother is good on the computer,' he said to me. 'Beat me a couple of times.'

'Richard!' Josephine sounded cross.

'Sorry, I was just trying to make him comfortable.'

'All right, but please, that deposition has to be done by this afternoon.'

'I'm on to it.' Richard left.

I wished he'd stay and chat to us. Anything to avoid me talking. I sipped my tea. My mouth thanked me. I took another sip.

'Now Julie, how old are you? What's your date of birth?'

'I'm fifteen. I was born the same day Indira Ghandi died.'

Josephine looked at me. 'Now I should be able to retrieve that date out of my file.'

I expected her to get up and look in the filing cabinet. Instead she looked at the ceiling. There was one of those fans going round and round, making a soft whirr.

'Correct me if I'm wrong, but I believe it was October thirty-first, nineteen eighty-four.'

Smart. I felt good all of a sudden. I had a smart lawyer. 'Yep, that's right.' I smiled at her. 'Mum used to go on and on about Mahatma Ghandi, being a pacifist and all.' I stopped myself. I wasn't going to say how stupid it all seemed now. Mum talking about non-violence when we lived in constant violence. Another irky feeling about Mum started creeping in.

'You went to the local high school?'

'Yep. Grade nine.'

'Did you like school?'

'Yeah.' I wasn't going to say more than I needed to.

'Well, now we get to the tricky bit. I have to ask you questions about your home life.'

'What sort of questions?'

'Probably pretty hard questions, Julie. You see the court wants to get some idea of your family life. You and Toby are the only ones to really ask.'

'Mum told us not to say anything to anyone, ever,' I said defiantly.

Josephine sighed. 'Julie, you're not the only one to live with violence at home.' She paused. 'In fact, it's quite common. Sometimes physical, sometimes verbal, sometimes worse. Most children are told not to tell anyone. It's wrong though, can you see that?' Josephine looked at me with those green eyes.

'Wrong. Why?'

'Everyone has a basic human right to live without fear and violence, this doesn't just mean the streets.

It means the home as well. For some reason people think it is something to be ashamed of, living with a violent parent or parents. Children take it on as if they're the cause of the violence. They're not. It's the adults' problems; children are the innocent victims, do you understand that?'

'That's what my counsellor said.' I felt numb.

'Your mother was wrong to expect you to keep the secret. I don't mean to sound harsh, but now she is dead and your father faces murder charges, there is even more reason for you and Toby to tell us about your family life. I know it is very hard to betray what you think were your mother's wishes but, I think given what's happened, your mother would expect you to speak honestly.'

I stared out the window, thinking. Even though Mum was dead, I still thought she'd kill me if I told a stranger about what it had been like at home. Why, after everything else, was this happening to me? Wasn't it enough that we had been through what we'd been through? Why did I have to talk about it? Why, why? It was so unfair. I looked at the clock. I'd been there half-an-hour already. God, if we kept going at this rate, I'd be here all day.

'Julie, I know that you suddenly have to unlearn pretty much a lifetime of being taught to keep your family's business private. Whatever it is.' She looked

186

at me. I nodded. 'Unfortunately you're in a situation that you can't control.' She smiled. I nodded again. 'The sooner you get this over and done with, and as soon as the court case is over, you'll be able to leave it all behind.'

'I don't know how to talk about it,' I said almost in tears, 'it's so hard to talk about.'

'Have you ever talked to anyone about it? Jean? Your counsellor?' Josephine asked, kindly.

'Not much. Toby and I talk about the house burning 'cause of all the things we lost.'

'Well, maybe we'll start from there. How did you feel when you heard the house had burnt down?'

I took a deep breath. I saw the burnt remains. I thought of Jesse, our dog. I finally mumbled. 'I couldn't believe it.'

'And your mother, and brother and sister dying?'

'Couldn't believe it.' I couldn't hold back the tears. They were trickling down my face. 'And Jesse,' I added.

'Jesse?'

'Our dog.' The dam burst. I was blubbering and there was nothing I could do to stop it. Josephine got up quickly and grabbed a packet of tissues.

'I'm sorry, I'm sorry,' I tried to say.

'It's okay.' She put her arm around me. 'Cry all you like. We'll have a little break. Would you like more tea?'

I nodded my head.

Josephine left the room. It gave me time to try and pull myself together. I was so embarrassed. Fancy bawling like that in front of a stranger. What would she think of me? Remember, breathe, I told myself trying to choke my sobs. There were all these saturated tissues in front of me. Gee, I didn't even use tissues unless they were recycled. Don't get me wrong. I don't mean dried out tissues, I mean made from recycled paper. I saw a bin and I dumped the wet tissues in.

Josephine came back with a fresh pot of tea. 'Feeling a bit better?' she asked.

'A bit.'

'Are you seeing your counsellor anytime between now and next week?' Josephine asked.

'No. She's on holiday till the end of the month.'

'Mm. That's a pity. I thought maybe if you talked over with her some of the things we've been talking about, it might help you feel safer about talking to me.'

I was confused. I mean I sort of felt safe with Josephine. I didn't want to remember. It hurt too much. I took a deep breath.

'I think I can do it. I know I have to, it's just hard not to cry that's all.'

'Crying is fine.'

'That's what my aunt says.'

'Do you think you are ready to begin again,' Josephine said softly.

'I'll try.'

'What do you remember most about your family life?'

I wiped my eyes. 'The fighting.'

'Was that often?'

'Always, ever since I can remember.'

'Did your father hit your mother?'

'He hit everybody.'

Josephine kept writing. 'How often did he hit you?'

'I can't remember, but he hit Mum and Toby more than me, he really had it in for Toby.'

'Did he hit with his open hand or a closed fist?'

'Mostly his fists, but he also used sticks, belts or even rope. Once he hit me with a board that had fallen off the chicken coop, but I used to run away or hide from him.'

'How often did he hit your mother?'

'It seemed like every day, but it wasn't.'

'How do you know?'

'Because sometimes he'd get drunk and stay in town at the pub.' I remembered other occasions when Dad wasn't home. 'Sometimes the cop would come out and take him away for the night and then bring him back in the morning.'

'That's interesting, did that happen often?'

'No, not really. It was only when Toby or I had rung him for the millionth time. Mostly he wouldn't even come, he'd say they'd sort it out. Sometimes we thought they might kill each other.' I shuddered. 'In the end, Dad did,' I said softly. 'I should have been there, I could have stopped him.' I put my head in my hands and willed myself not to cry.

'No, Julie, don't think like that. He may have killed you all. Now for the rest of his life he knows he has two children who may never be able to forgive him, who he won't know as they grow up, who he won't share happy times with, and you have a whole life in front of you. You can make yourself a good life.' Josephine smiled at me.

'I rang Kidsline once. You know where you can talk to someone anonymously about what's going on,' I paused, 'but I hung up, I was too scared and Mum was only just outside and I was worried that she'd come in and catch me.'

'That's a shame, they may have been able to offer you help.'

I looked at her. 'Do you think so? I thought they didn't know who you were.'

'They don't, but what I mean is that they may have been able to tell you other places you could get practical help, even for your mother and father.'

Josephine asked lots of other questions and I was getting tired. I started fidgeting and squirming in my seat.

'Maybe we ought to stop now,' Josephine put her pen down. I noticed she'd written more than ten pages of stuff. Did I say all of that? 'It's nearly lunch time.'

I looked at the clock on her desk and was amazed at how fast the time had gone. We walked out of the office. Toby was still on the computer and I was pretty sure Richard raced back to his desk when we came out.

'I think I'll order some lunch,' Josephine said.

I went over to Toby.

'What was it like?' he asked.

'Hard, really hard, but you have to tell her everything, Toby.'

'Everything?'

'Yep. They aren't secrets any more because they're bad secrets. You can tell her anything you want, she's great.'

'Did you tell her everything?'

'Nearly.' I looked behind me. Josephine and Richard had their heads bent over some papers. 'I didn't tell her about the night with the gun.'

'You mean when he shot at Mum, but missed and we didn't know if he meant it or not?'

'Yeah. That night.'

'Why not?'

'I just couldn't, it wouldn't come out.'

'Do you think I should tell her?'

'Tell her what you want, Toby. You might be like me, not able to say some things,' I sniffed.

We looked at each other. Gee, I loved my brother. I suddenly hugged him.

'Don't. Get off,' he said

'Toby, I love you.'

'Shut up, what's the matter with you?' he said.

'Toby if we don't say it to each other we might forget.'

'Crap!'

'Don't be like that, Toby. Please?' I could feel tears coming.

He looked away and I let go of him. Josephine called him. He looked at me and I could tell he was frightened. His pupils were huge and I remembered how Dad told me that's why you never looked in the eyes of a snake if you were scared, because they could see fear in the size of your pupils, he said dogs could too. I didn't believe him.

'It's okay.' I grabbed his hand. 'Tell her what a bullshitting bully Dad was.'

Then to my surprise he hugged me and said, 'I love you sis.' He walked slowly behind Josephine, looking back once. I whispered good luck.

Aunt Jean appeared, just as Josephine's office door closed.

'Do you want to go somewhere for lunch?' she asked me.

I didn't really want to go out in public but my stomach was rumbling and I suddenly felt really hungry. All that talking and crying, I suppose.

'I could eat a horse,' I said.

'There's a little restaurant two streets away that does a good baked horse with baby carrots in a bed of straw,' Richard said, laughing.

Was he for real? God, I couldn't eat horse. Aunt Jean laughed and grabbed my hand.

'I think a nice pasta might do the trick,' Aunt Jean said, smiling at Richard.

Outside it felt like rain wasn't far away. The air was heavy and the sky disorganised.

'How did you go?' Aunt Jean asked as we walked.

'It was hard at first, but then I just sort of burst and told her heaps.'

'Josephine is a very good person and a very good lawyer,' Aunt Jean said.

'And smart,' I said.

Aunt Jean smiled. 'And smart.'

We went into this restaurant. It was quite crowded but we found a table.

'Do you mind ordering for me, Aunt Jean. I can't decide, there are too many choices.'

Aunt Jean had a knack of knowing what was delicious. I ate as if I hadn't eaten for days. I even fitted in this dessert called Tortoni. I felt kilos heavier as we left.

'Maybe we could go to the library,' Aunt Jean said, 'I've got my mobile so when Toby finishes, Josephine will ring.'

'Great. Maybe we can find a book on dreams.'

The library was huge. I thought Mrs Thompson, the librarian from back home, would have been in heaven if she came here.

'It's so big,' I said, staring at the millions of books.

'Yes, it's a great library.'

We walked up to the enquiries counter, where I filled in a form and became a member. Unbelievable. I had access to all of this. Maybe I wouldn't become a world champion surfer. Maybe I'd become a librarian, I thought, as we climbed the stairs.

Time seemed to fly by. There were more books on dreams than there were books in the library back home. Aunt Jean showed me how to use the computer to narrow down the choices of books I might want to borrow. We made a list and then found them on the shelves.

Aunt Jean's phone rang and a few people gave her a dirty look. Toby was ready. I was surprised that it was three o'clock already. An hour till Ruby arrived. I started feeling excited and nervous about seeing her again. Had I changed, since I moved here?

We walked back to Josephine's office in silence. The streets were less busy now all the workers had finished their lunchtime. It was the shoppers now, bustling along. We walked up the steps and into the building.

'Oh, here you are,' Josephine said. Toby and I looked at each other. I could tell he'd been crying. I wanted to rush to him, but I didn't. I don't know why. Maybe I was too embarrassed in front of the others. I don't know. I smiled at him. He sort of smiled back. He was all right.

'I don't think we have time today to talk to you both,' Josephine said, more at Aunt Jean than us.

'No, I don't think so. We've got to meet Julie's friend in less than an hour,' Aunt Jean replied, looking at her watch.

'How about we make another appointment now? It won't be so hard the next time, I hope.' Josephine smiled at us.

I just smiled and nodded. Richard brought a diary over and he ran his finger down the page. 'How about Monday fortnight, same time?' he said cheerfully. Toby and I looked at each other. That was long enough away to not think about it.

'Fine,' we said at the same time. Richard wrote it in the book.

'I just want a few words with Josephine,' Aunt Jean said. 'I'll only be a couple of minutes.'

I knew Josephine couldn't tell Aunt Jean much. Client privilege, they called it. I thought she might just want to find out if we said anything at all. Toby and I sat down at this little table. We both picked up a magazine. I couldn't read what was in front of me. 'Did you tell her everything?' I whispered.

'Mostly,' he said. 'I'll tell you later.'

Aunt Jean came out.

'Let's go,' she said. 'Thanks Jo, thanks,' They hugged and kissed each other goodbye.

We left the office and walked along the street. We're going to meet Ruby was all I could think about. I wanted to skip up the street, but restrained myself.

CHAPTER 12

Wednesday Evening

We were back at the flat. We'd come straight home from the station. Ruby and I had squealed as we hugged each other. It was so good to see her. We both kept talking the whole way back in the car. Mostly Ruby telling me all the gossip about my friends in the country, that is when she wasn't expressing amazement at the people in the streets, the buildings, the shops, the sheer size of the city. Every now and then I noticed Aunt Jean and Toby look at each other with raised eyebrows. No one asked them to listen.

I told her what I felt like the first time I went in to the city. We laughed. Aunt Jean made us all a cool drink. Ruby and I took ours up to the roof. I wanted to show her everything.

'Do you want to go for a swim, later?' I asked.

'I've never been in the sea,' Ruby answered.

'You'll love it,' I said. 'I'm going to learn to surf.'

'Deadly.'

'I'm going to be the world champion, one day,' I said, puffing my chest out.

'Go for it, girl. You got the lungs for it, I've heard you yell, remember?'

We laughed. It was like we'd seen each other yesterday, not months ago.

'Hope you don't get homesick,' I said suddenly.

Ruby stared out to sea. 'I'm a bit homesick already, but don't worry girl, it's a blackfella curse.'

'What do you mean?'

'Oh, you know, we miss our own country, coz we know it so well. It's a whole story if you know what I mean. When I come to some other fella's country, I feel a bit strange, you know, in my blood. If we stay away too long we get sick, happens to all of us, and I reckon that's why there are so many unhappy blackfellas, coz they're in the wrong country, away from their stories.'

'Are you feeling sick now?'

'Don't be silly girl, I've only been here an hour,' Ruby laughed. 'I'm just a bit homesick for Mum and everyone, I'll get used to it, don't worry. I'm here to have fun and you've got to show me everything.'

'I hope you're going to like it here?'

'I already do. I've got to visit some of Mum and Dad's rels in Redfern sometime,' Ruby said seriously.

'It's easy with all the trains to get anywhere.'

'I have to real soon.'

'Maybe tomorrow,' I said, 'we could get a bus to the city or a bus to the junction and catch a train.' I was enthusiastic.

'Maybe. Some of them don't live in Redfern, they live all over, but I don't want to spend the whole time with them, you know being dragged round being introduced to aunties and uncles and cousins and god knows.' Ruby looked at me. 'You're my excuse out of there.'

We both laughed. 'I don't know if I've been called an excuse before. Mm, it may take some getting used to.' I rubbed my chin. Then I heard in my head the day my father said to me, 'You're a poor excuse for a girl.' I must have been about five.

'What's up?'

I looked at Ruby. 'Sometimes my Dad comes into my head out of nowhere. I don't want to think about him. I don't want to be like him.'

'Jules, you aren't anything like him. He's got whiskers and you know what,' she said laughing. I laughed with her and we both looked out to sea.

'What's happening with court and all that?'

I knew it wasn't easy for her to ask. 'We saw our lawyer today. The trial is starting on the sixth of June.'

'Do you have to go?'

'Yeah. Toby and I have to give evidence.' I picked a leaf from the herb nearest me, and crushed it between my fingers and a lemon scent rose to my nostrils. 'Our lawyer is hoping we can do it by video, you know, so we don't have to actually be there.'

'Jesus, I hope you don't have to be in the same room as that mongrel.'

I was shocked at the anger in her voice.

'Me neither. I don't want to see him again as long as I live.'

'Why would you?'

'That's right. Why would I?'

'How's Toby?'

'Oh, you know. Up and down. He handles it differently I think. I still cry a lot and still think I don't believe it, and I'm going to wake up from this nightmare, any minute.'

'Oh Jules. Gee, I wish there was something I could do, you know, something to make you feel better.'

'Ruby, you being here is the best thing that's happened in ages.' I hugged her and I think she was a bit surprised. 'Let's go have a swim. I'm sick of talking about it today, I mean hours with the lawyer. I just want to get him out of my head.'

'Bastard,' Ruby said.

As we were walking down the stairs I thought of

the mystery uncle. Should I tell her now? No, I'll tell her after our swim.

'We're going for a swim,' I said. 'Do you want to come Toby?' I was feeling generous. I didn't really want him hanging out with Ruby and I, but he wasn't allowed to go to the beach on his own.

'Great,' he said as he raced off to get his bathers.

'I'll get some tea together. We could have it on the roof, when you get back.'

'Thanks, Aunt Jean.' I even went and hugged her. It was like I had a hugging virus or something.

We crossed the road.

'Wow, it's all so big,' Ruby said. 'So many bloody people, haven't they got homes to go to? Look at 'em all.'

'You sort of get used to it,' I said.

'Don't reckon I ever could get used to so many strangers,' Ruby replied shaking her head as a bloke with purple and green hair and earrings did cartwheels in front of us, saying sorry, sorry. She looked at me. I laughed. 'What was that?' she said.

'That's what I'm going to look like next time you visit,' said Toby. What a clown. He was the first to nudge me and point when different-looking people than we'd seen in the country, went by.

'Sure, I'll believe that when I see it,' I said to him with a push.

'Well maybe not purple and green,' he looked thoughtful, 'maybe purple and yellow.'

We all laughed as we ran down the steps to the sand. The beach wasn't crowded to me, but Ruby thought it was. She wanted to find a place that was as far from any near naked body as possible.

I told her about the flags and how we had to swim between them.

'I don't know if I want to go in,' Ruby said when I'd finished going on about rips and undertows and dumpers. I didn't mention sharks, but Toby did. I could have strangled him. 'What would Mum say if I didn't come back?'

'You'll be fine, Ruby. Don't worry I'll look after you,' I said. 'You don't even have to go in deep. It feels great. It's so different to fresh water. Come on, Ruby. You can't come all this way to the sea and not put your foot in.'

'S'pose not,' Ruby mumbled.

'Come on, just feel the water.'

'All right, but any sharks or things and I'm outta here,' Ruby said.

Toby raced in and plunged beneath the waves.

'Show off,' Ruby called after him.

We walked to the edge. Ruby jumped back at first, but then she just went for it.

'It's wicked,' Ruby laughed, her eyes gleaming.

I told her about body-surfing and there was enough of a swell for her to try it. It was fantastic. I was so happy. My very own friend. Someone I could whisper with in the dark. Someone to sit on the bed with and laugh. I started squealing and jumping up and down. Ruby and Toby joined in. If anyone had seen us I think they would have called for the Mental Health Authority. We looked crazy.

Ruby and I got tired of body-surfing and the waves. We made our way back to the sand. Toby stayed in. Ruby was a natural.

'Gee, you were good, Ruby,' I thought about the story I'd heard about how some white people saw some Aborigines body-surfing off the break at Ben Buckler when they'd lived here as a tribe, and thought if they could do it, so could the whites. I wondered whether to tell Ruby about it and thought I'd tell her later.

'That was fantastic, Jules. You must love living here, like I love living at the waterhole,' Ruby said, drying her long black hair.

'It's great,' I said. 'You know its weird in a way. Toby and I are so lucky to have Aunt Jean, the beach.' I stopped, trying to figure out what I wanted to say. 'It's sad that it took losing Mum to get here. You know she lived here when she was a kid.'

Ruby nodded her head and stayed quiet, waiting for me to say whatever I wanted to say.

'It reminds me how my Mum used to say, Every cloud has a silver lining, you know how mothers say those things.'

'Yeah, Mum always says, You can't kill a snake till sundown.'

I laughed. 'Well, you know after she was dead and everything,' I paused, 'well sometimes, I thought I could hear her voice saying that about the silver lining, you know.'

Ruby knew and put her arm around me. I took a deep breath.

'Well, it's a bit like that I suppose, I thought everything was bad, bad. You know that deep hole you spiral in to and you never get to the bottom, just go round and round in your head, you know?'

Ruby looked at me. 'Yeah, I know.'

'Then we had to come here. We had nowhere else to go and it's great. I love it. I love Aunt Jean. I love the peace, I love that she doesn't yell at us or punish us cruelly for nothing, you know.'

'You had it bad with your Dad, didn't you?'

'Yeah. Bad. I've never talked about it before, but today I had to tell the lawyer things and I feel better.' It was amazing but I did. 'It's like a weight off. Not keeping other people's ugly secrets.'

'Did the lawyer say that?'

'She said some secrets are actually crimes.'

'Yeah, I know,' Ruby looked sad all of a sudden. I wondered what she was thinking about.

'I've got a ripper secret for you though,' I said, hoping to bring her back to me. I didn't want to make her sad, talking about my life. 'You won't believe it.'

Toby came racing up. He shook his wet hair on me. 'Toby,' I screamed.

'Sorry.' He was showing off in front of Ruby. Oh, oh. Did my little brother have a crush on Ruby? Whoa there. This would be worth heaps. I scrunched my face up in glee.

'Toby, I think you better behave a bit more maturely in front of my friend.' I gave him my evil look. 'You wouldn't want to give Ruby a bad impression, now would you?' I grinned at him. 'Would you?'

He went the colour of a tomato, but it shut him up.

'I'll tell you later,' I said to Ruby, quietly.

'You better,' Ruby said.

'You won't believe it,' I said.

We gathered our things up and crossed the road. I half-expected a strange man to jump out, but nothing happened. We got back to the flat. Aunt Jean had prepared a feast.

'You kids shower, then we can carry this to the roof,' Aunt Jean said, as we came in to the kitchen.

I hoped she wasn't going to call us kids all the time in front of Ruby. I thought of saying we aren't kids, but didn't want to spoil my good feeling. I'd let Aunt Jean get away with it this time. Only this time. Next time . . . well watch out.

'Did you enjoy the beach, Ruby?'

'It was great um . . .' Ruby looked at me.

'Call me Jean.'

'Yeah. Okay um Jean. It sounds funny without an auntie in front of it though,' Ruby smiled. 'I mean I'm so used to you being called Aunt Jean.' Ruby looked at Aunt Jean as if she needed help with this conversation.

'Call me auntie, if it helps,' Aunt Jean laughed.

'It's easier for me,' Ruby said.

'Do you want first shower?' I asked Ruby.

'Yeah,'

I showed her the bathroom and got her a towel.

After our showers we carried food upstairs.

'When are you going to tell me,' Ruby asked.

'When we get a bit of privacy,' I answered, indicating Aunt Jean.

On our next trip, the phone rang and Aunt Jean

went to answer it. Toby was still in the shower. You could hear him singing, badly. Ruby and I got the rest of the food and some plates. 'Let's hurry, I might get a chance to tell you.'

We put the food and plates down.

'You won't believe it,' I said.

'You've said that before,' Ruby answered. 'Get on with it.'

'We have an uncle,' I said triumphantly.

'Big deal, I've got hundreds,' Ruby laughed. 'Is that the big secret?'

I was a bit offended. 'We didn't even know we had one. He's Dad's brother.'

'You didn't know? It happens with us all the time, I didn't know it happened with you gubbas. Was he stolen or something?'

I told her about the photograph and what Mum had said. 'He was banished.'

'Banished?'

'Yeah, you know kicked out, never to return.'

'Hell!' Ruby was amazed. 'Gee, our people had no choice, their kids were just stolen.' Ruby looked thoughtful. 'Banishment was used as punishment in our law if someone did something bad. I mean really bad like rape or something. They weren't ever allowed back to their country. I didn't know you whitefellas did it.'

'Well, his father kicked him out forever when my father was in Vietnam.' I wondered how to say the next bit. 'Um, you wanna know what he did?'

'Blood oath, I want to know.'

'He fell in love with an Aboriginal woman.'

'You're gammin?'

'No. He wanted to marry her and his father chucked him out. She was pregnant,' I looked at Ruby. 'Her name was Aloma.'

Ruby went white. I mean, I know she's black but she looked like she went pale.

'You mean Wayne?' she said.

'God, you know him?'

'Aloma's one of my bloody cousins.'

'What?'

'Yeah. Aloma and Wayne. They aren't together any more.' Ruby looked thoughtful. 'You know what this means, don't you?'

'No.' I was dumbfounded. What did it mean?

'Your cousins are my cousins.'

We looked at each other. In a funny way now we were family.

'Oh Ruby, that means you and I are sort of cousins.'

'Yeah, sort of,' Ruby said, grabbing my hand and giving it a twist.

'Didn't you ever know who Wayne was?' I asked.

'I was too young, I reckon. I remember him a little bit, when I was about five or something. Gee, Mum would know.'

'Do you think your Mum knew who I was? You know, Wayne's niece.'

'I bet you she bloody did. You know what it's like in our mob, we're all related and we know everything about each other.' Ruby paused. 'I don't believe it.'

'I told you, you wouldn't,' I said.

'I remember he used to go off working or something and one time he never came back. I remember something going on and never seeing him again.' Ruby looked far away. 'How about that, you never knew.'

Tears came to my eyes. 'Why didn't Mum tell me the truth?'

'She might have, one day. You never know.' Ruby looked like she regretted saying that. 'Maybe she was waiting for you to be a bit older,' Ruby spoke quickly. 'That's what happens with Mum. She says when you're old enough, I'll tell you.'

I knew Ruby was trying to make me feel better. I had to make an effort. 'Yeah. You're probably right. Mum was so scared of Dad that she'd practically do anything he told her. The meaner he got, the meeker Mum got.' I stared at the cold sea. The never-ending sea. Families, I thought. What goes wrong? Why do people who love each other, hate each other?

'I can't believe it, cuz,' Ruby said grabbing my arm.

'Cuz.' I smiled back into her eyes.

Aunt Jean and Toby appeared on the roof.

'I told Ruby about Wayne and guess what we're sort of cousins,' I said proudly.

'Cousins,' Toby said. All thoughts of Ruby being his girlfriend evaporated.

'Aloma is one of Ruby's cousins.'

Aunt Jean looked surprised. 'You know Wayne?'

'Only a bit,' Ruby answered. 'I haven't seen him for years. I hardly remember him.'

There was silence and I could see Toby out of the corner of my eye, staring at his new sort-of cousin.

'Well actually, that was him on the phone.'

I looked alarmed. I sought Toby. We stared at each other. Wayne is never going to give up, I thought.

'I told him, at this stage, you don't want to meet him.'

I looked at Ruby. After all he was sort of her cousin.

'I don't,' said Toby and he folded his arms and leant back on the chair.

'Don't do that,' Aunt Jean said, 'it breaks the chairs.'

I thought he was going to chuck it, with the look on his face, but instead he said, 'Sorry.'

'I don't know,' I said. Ruby stayed quiet. Aunt Jean started to toss the salad. Night noises rose up from the street.

We ate in silence. I knew Ruby was a bit embarrassed because she didn't know what some of the food was. I helped her, remembering what it was like for me at first with the hundred-and-fifty types of lettuce when we'd only ever seen one, before coming here.

'If you like, after we've eaten, we could go down to the beach and watch the moon rise. It'll be full tonight. We could have a swim,' Aunt Jean said.

It sounded great. I'd never swum in the dark before.

'What about sharks?' Toby said. Trust him, always the sharks.

'Don't worry about that,' Aunt Jean said laughing. 'We won't go out deep.'

'What do you reckon, Ruby?' I asked.

'If you're game, girl, so am I,' Ruby looked at me. I knew she was thinking, you first. I laughed.

The beach was practically empty. It was still light but the sky was changing from day to night. Lovers

211

walked by. The most out-of-shape people you could imagine jogged by, and we all laughed. Why did they bother? I thought. We sat down on our towels.

'Do you think you'll go in?' I asked Ruby.

'After you.'

'I'll race you.'

We took off and dived in. It felt divine. I opened my eyes under the water and thought I saw a mermaid. I saw Toby's legs. I swam for them. I grabbed them and dragged him under. We both spluttered to the surface.

'You almost scared me to death,' he said. 'I thought you were a shark.'

I laughed. 'Got you,' I screamed at him.

'Right,' he said, and swam away. 'Till the next time,' he called out when he was beyond my reach. I couldn't be bothered chasing him.

Ruby swam up. 'The sea is great,' she said.

'Fabulous. Tell the others back home won't you.'

'You bet. They'll all be packing their bags to come and live with you.'

'No, don't do that. This is mine,' I waved my arms about. 'All mine.'

'You whitefellas,' Ruby laughed as she swam away.

'The moon, the moon,' Aunt Jean called out.

Sure enough, this enormous light appeared on

the horizon. Little by little, the arc of light increased until it was this great big fiery ball.

'Wow. I never knew the moon got so big,' Toby said.

'It's enormous,' I answered.

We watched as it rose slowly in the sky. It turned into a smaller and smaller ball the higher it got. If you hadn't seen it for yourself, you wouldn't have thought it was the same rising moon.

'Time to go home,' Aunt Jean finally said.

I felt tired, so tired. The apartment was cooler than it was outside. I had made up a bed for Ruby in my room.

'I'm going to bed,' Aunt Jean said when we got home. 'I hope you are comfortable Ruby.'

'Yeah, great. Don't worry about me, Auntie Jean,' Ruby said. Aunt Jean laughed. I wasn't sure if Ruby was being a bit cheeky or what?

I hoped Ruby would be comfortable. If she wasn't, she could have my bed. I brushed my teeth and got into my nightie. I had a quick look in the mirror to see if I was still me. I was, but I was a happier me than the one I'd seen in the mirror this morning.

'It's a great room,' Ruby said as I got into bed.

'I love it, especially listening to the sea at night,' I replied.

'Gee, the traffic's noisy but.'

213

'You get used to it. I sort of don't even hear it now.' I turned out the lamp.

I lay there thinking about the day. 'I hope you like it here, Ruby,' I said to the darkness.

'I reckon, I will,' her sleepy voice said back.

'Ruby?'

'Mm.'

'Do you reckon I should meet Uncle Wayne?'

'I don't know girl. It's up to you.'

'I just don't know. I mean he doesn't sound like Dad and he is blood.'

'I reckon I would be curious, but it's different for me. I still meet relatives all over the place, even close blood ones that I'd never heard of before.'

'Do you?'

'Yeah. You know the ones that were stolen and lost who come back sometimes.'

'There's so much sadness in your people,' I said, softly.

'Oceans girl, oceans,' Ruby replied. 'But hey, let's not talk about that, let's think of something happy before we go to sleep.'

'Oh Ruby, sometimes I wonder if I'll ever be happy.'

'Oh Jules, don't say that.'

'Well, you know, the court case. I don't know if I can handle it, I haven't told any of the girls here, you know, about Dad and that.'

'Shit girl, the judge will stop them saying your names and that, won't he?'

'I don't know. Something about the right of the public to know or something, that's what the lawyer said. The judge may stop our names, but it doesn't happen often in this sort of crime.'

'Why have the public the right to know your business? Sounds suss to me.'

'I don't know. You know, I've never thought about it before, but those people you see on TV, you know the families of murder victims, it must be horrible.'

'You could disguise yourself, so people don't recognise you,' Ruby offered helpfully.

'Our names?'

'Gawd, could be millions of people with your names.'

'We'll have to take time off school at the time of the trial.'

'Say you're sick, paint spots on or something.'

I laughed. 'I don't want to worry about it now. I've got months to worry. Like you said, be happy before I go to sleep.'

'That's what me Mum reckons. Go to sleep happy, wake up happy.'

'Is it true?' I asked.

'Works for me, girl.'

'Well, I am so happy that you are here, Ruby. I'm happy that we'll be able to do things and go places together.' I thought for a moment. 'I'm so happy, you're my best friend.'

'Me too, Jules, goodnight.'

'Goodnight Ruby, happy dreams.' I shut my eyes. The sea kept on roaring. I heard Ruby's breathing change. I knew she'd already fallen asleep. I knew I ought to stop worrying about the court case, Dad and everything else. It sometimes was hard just to stop thinking bad thoughts. Happy thoughts, I thought. Happy thoughts and I can worry about everything else tomorrow.

Epilogue

The holidays are over. It was really hard saying goodbye to Ruby. We both cried at the station. Jasmine and Phoebe had got a surprise meeting Ruby. I hadn't told them she was Aboriginal. I hadn't thought it was important. They all liked each other, which was a relief. Phoebe and Jasmine said she was the first Aboriginal person they'd really talked to. I was sort of surprised. There were Aboriginal students at school, but I noticed they pretty much hung around together. There wasn't much mixing. Some individuals mixed, but most of the kids seemed to hang out with those most like them.

Ruby and I had surfing lessons. Aunt Jean paid and we hired surfboards. It was even better than I thought it would be. Ruby was good at it straight away. She said it was the best thing she'd ever done in her life. I agreed. I'm saving up for my own board.

The court case is still months away. I am dreading it. Dad has written us a letter. It is sitting on top of the fridge, unopened. Uncle Wayne rang a few times. Toby ended up meeting him when he went back there for his holiday. They'd gone fishing on the Birrie River. Toby loved it and said Uncle Wayne was all right. He'd even helped Uncle Wayne start building the new house on our old farm.

I stared out the window. The scene has become so familiar. It almost feels like home. It is my home, I thought. This is it; this is where I live. I'll never look out on sheep and red dirt again. Just a boulevard of people and the ocean. Could be worse. I thought of the pictures on TV of the kids in Timor. Could be worse, I said and blew my breath on the window and drew the infinity sign.